開場白①

Would you like to hear an interesting story?

It's one I think you will like.

It starts out like this.

開場白❷

I want to tell you a story.

I like it very much.

It goes like this.

開場白❸

Want to hear a story?

I think it's pretty good.

It teaches a nice lesson.

開場白❹

I know a fun story.

I want you to hear it.

It begins like this.

序言

「**用英文說故事①**」是專為中國人設計的英文故事書。推出這本書的目標，就是要讓大家知道，學英文其實很簡單，只要從生動有趣的英文故事開始，每個人都可以輕鬆開口說英文。

這本書非常特別，可以看、可以聽、還可以讓你開口說給別人聽。媽媽可以在床邊，用英文講故事給小孩聽，小孩可以一邊看著圖，一邊聽媽媽說故事。你也可以在閒暇時，把CD拿出來播給自己聽，讓故事的情節，推動你一篇一篇地看下去，從這本書開始，英文將成為你的好朋友。

「**用英文說故事①**」精選三十則短篇英文故事，有的故事很有趣，有的故事可以教你很多東西，每一篇都值得一讀再讀。本書是採用中英對照的方式，每一篇都有中文翻譯，而且針對稍難的字彙，還附加註解。另外，每一頁都有生動活潑的彩色圖片，適合全家大小一起讀。

俗話說：「萬事起頭難。」學語言也是，大家都不喜歡難的東西，所以我們要從簡單易懂的故事開始學起，讓你對英文自然而然產生興趣。當你把一個故事聽很多遍之後，你就可以開始試著說英文故事給朋友聽，有了聽眾之後，你說的英文故事會更精采。

劉　毅

CONTENTS

1. The Hidden Treasure
   藏 寶 …… 1-1
2. The Clever Servant
   聰明的僕人 …… 2-1
3. Polly's Dream
   波莉之夢 …… 3-1
4. The Donkey in the Lion's Skin
   披著獅皮的驢 …… 4-1
5. In a Train Car
   車廂中 …… 5-1
6. I Am Not a Bear
   我不是熊 …… 6-1
7. It's a Boy or a Girl
   男孩還是女孩 …… 7-1
8. The Farmer, His Horse, and His Son
   農夫、馬和他的兒子 …… 8-1
9. A Slip of the Tongue
   說溜了嘴 …… 9-1
10. A Tall Hat
   高帽子 …… 10-1
11. Interesting Words
   有趣的字 …… 11-1
12. The Girl in the Store
   商店裡的女孩 …… 12-1
13. Nature Can Help Us Learn Many Secrets
   大自然可以使我們得知許多秘密 …… 13-1
14. Unlucky Man
   倒楣的人 …… 14-1
15. Maybe Your Friend Is in That Carpet
   也許你的朋友在那塊地毯裡 …… 15-1

16. Fishing
釣　魚 ………………………………… 16-1
17. He Also Needed It
他也需要它 ………………………………… 17-1
18. How We Get Day and Night
日夜的由來 ………………………………… 18-1
19. Friendship Is a Treasure
友誼是很珍貴的 ………………………………… 19-1
20. Two Hours Too Early!
早兩個小時！ ………………………………… 20-1
21. A Most Forgetful Couple
非常健忘的夫婦 ………………………………… 21-1
22. The Snake Translator
蛇翻譯員 ………………………………… 22-1
23. Heads or Tails, You Lose
不論正面或反面，你都是輸 ………………………………… 23-1
24. The Face That Launched a Thousand Ships
一張發動千軍萬馬的臉 ………………………………… 24-1
25. The Amazing Earthworm
不可思議的蚯蚓 ………………………………… 25-1
26. The Next Speaker Listens Well
下一位演講者最專心聽 ………………………………… 26-1
27. The Indians Were First
印地安人最早來 ………………………………… 27-1
28. Paul Bunyan—an American Legend
保羅・班揚—美國傳奇人物 ………………………………… 28-1
29. No Sense of Direction
沒有方向感 ………………………………… 29-1
30. A Lily in the Kitchen
廚房裡的百合花 ………………………………… 30-1

1. The Hidden Treasure

Once upon a time, there was a very old farmer. He had worked hard all his life.

---

hidden (ˈhɪdn̩)

once upon a time

hard (hɑrd)

treasure (ˈtrɛʒɚ)

farmer (ˈfɑrmɚ)

all** one's **life

He had three young sons, but they were all very lazy. He wanted them to become skilled farmers.

---

young 〔 jʌŋ 〕 son 〔 sʌn 〕
lazy 〔ˈlezɪ 〕 become 〔 bɪˈkʌm 〕
skilled 〔 skɪld 〕

One day, the farmer got very sick, and he realized he was dying. He called his sons to him and said,

---

one day

sick [sɪk]

die [daɪ]

get [gɛt]

realize [ˈriəˌlaɪz]

"Boys, I will be leaving you soon. There is a lot of gold hidden in the fields. Dig for it and find it. Everything you discover is yours."

---

leave [liv]	soon [sun]
a lot of	gold [gold]
fields [fildz]	dig [dɪg]
find [faɪnd]	
discover [dɪ'skʌvɚ]	

After the farmer was dead, the three boys searched for the gold in the fields. They had no idea where the special treasure was. They dug in every possible place. They dug and dug, but they still found no gold, and yet they turned up all the fields extremely well.

---

dead 〔 dɛd 〕

have no idea

possible 〔ˈpɑsəbl̩ 〕

turn up

search 〔 sɜtʃ 〕

special 〔ˈspɛʃəl 〕

and yet

extremely 〔 ɪkˈstrimlɪ 〕

The next autumn, they had an excellent harvest. When the three sons got so much money after they sold the grain, they came to realize what their father's words meant — there's gold hidden in the ground; dig for it. The real treasure was what they learned from working hard.

---

next [nɛkst]
autumn [′ɔtəm]
excellent [′ɛksḷənt]
harvest [′hɑrvɪst]
sell [sɛl]
grain [gren]
come to V.
words [wɝdz]
mean [min]
ground [graʊnd]
real [′riəl]

1. The Hidden Treasure

藏 寶

中文翻譯

Once upon a time, there was a very old farmer. He had worked hard all his life. He had three young sons, but they were all very lazy. He wanted them to become skilled farmers.

從前有個很老的農夫，他辛苦工作了一輩子。他有三個年輕的兒子，但他們都很懶散。老農夫想要他們成爲有技巧的農夫。

One day, the farmer got very sick, and he realized he was dying. He called his sons to him and said, "Boys, I will be leaving you soon. There is a lot of gold hidden in the fields. Dig for it and find it. Everything you discover is yours."

有一天，老農夫病得很重，他知道自己快死了。他把兒子叫到身邊，並說道：「孩子們，我快要離你們而去了。田裏藏著很多黃金。去把它們挖出來。找到就是你們的。」

** ———

hidden〔ˈhɪdn̩〕*adj.* 隱藏的　treasure〔ˈtrɛʒɚ〕*n.* 寶藏
once upon a time 從前　***all** one's **life*** 終生　lazy〔ˈlezɪ〕*adj.* 懶惰的
skilled〔skɪld〕*adj.* 有技巧的　***get very sick*** 病得很重
realize〔ˈriəˌlaɪz〕*v.* 知道　die〔daɪ〕*v.* 死　soon〔sun〕*adv.* 很快地
gold〔gold〕*n.* 黃金　hide〔haɪd〕*v.* 隱藏　fields〔fildz〕*n.pl.* 田地
dig〔dɪg〕*v.* 挖掘　discover〔dɪˈskʌvɚ〕*v.* 發現

After the farmer was dead, the three boys searched for the gold in the fields. They had no idea where the special treasure was. They dug in every possible place. They dug and dug, but they still found no gold, and yet they turned up all the fields extremely well.

老農夫死後，三個兒子便到田裏去找黃金。他們不知道那個特別的寶藏在哪裡。他們挖遍了每個可能的地方。他們挖呀挖，但並沒有發現任何黃金，可是他們卻將田裡所有的土都翻得很好。

The next autumn, they had an excellent harvest. When the three sons got so much money after they sold the grain, they came to realize what their father's words meant —— there's gold hidden in the ground; dig for it. The real treasure was what they learned from working hard.

次年秋天，他們的收成很好。三個兒子將穀物賣了之後，賺了許多錢，他們這才瞭解父親所說的 ——「田裏藏著金子；把它們挖出來」的含意。眞正的寶藏，就是他們從努力工作中，所學到的東西。

** ————————————————

dead〔dɛd〕*adj.* 死的　search〔sɝtʃ〕*v.* 尋找　***have no idea*** 不知道
and yet 但是　***turn up*** 翻掘　possible〔ˈpɑsəbl̩〕*adj.* 可能的
extremely〔ɪkˈstrimlɪ〕*adv.* 非常地　autumn〔ˈɔtəm〕*n.* 秋天
excellent〔ˈɛksl̩ənt〕*adj.* 極好的　harvest〔ˈhɑrvɪst〕*n.* 收成
get〔gɛt〕*v.* 賺得　sell〔sɛl〕*v.* 賣　grain〔gren〕*n.* 穀物
come to V. 開始　words〔wɝdz〕*n. pl.* 話
mean〔min〕*v.* 意思是　ground〔graʊnd〕*n.* 土地
real〔ˈriəl〕*adj.* 眞正的

2. The Clever Servant

Here's an old story. A wealthy man wanted to make a journey to a faraway town.

---

clever〔ˈklɛvɚ〕

servant〔ˈsɝvənt〕

wealthy〔ˈwɛlθɪ〕

journey〔ˈdʒɝnɪ〕

make a journey

faraway〔ˈfɑrəˈwe〕

town〔taʊn〕

He was a businessman. He wanted to take products to sell. He also planned to take gold to buy things with. He

decided to take ten servants with him. They would carry the goods to sell and the food to eat on the journey.

---

businessman [ˈbɪznɪsˌmæn]
product [ˈprɑdʌkt]
plan [plæn]
decide [dɪˈsaɪd]
goods [gʊdz]
sell [sɛl]
gold [gold]
carry [ˈkærɪ]
food [fud]

He was a kindhearted man. He said to one of his servants, "You are the shortest, the thinnest and the weakest of all my servants. You cannot carry a heavy bundle. You must choose the lightest bundle to carry."

---

kindhearted (ˈkaɪndˈhɑrtɪd)

short (ʃɔrt)

thin (θɪn)

weak (wik)

heavy (ˈhɛvɪ)

bundle (ˈbʌndḷ)

choose (tʃuz)

light (laɪt)

The servant thanked his master. He pointed to the largest bundle. This was the fruit and bread to eat on the journey.

---

thank〔θæŋk〕
master〔ˈmæstɚ〕
point〔pɔɪnt〕
point to
large〔lɑrdʒ〕
fruit〔frut〕
bread〔brɛd〕

"You are foolish," said his master. "That is the biggest and heaviest bundle." But the servant picked up the bundle cheerfully and the trip began.

---

foolish (ˈfulɪʃ)
cheerfully (ˈtʃɪrfəlɪ)
begin (bɪˈgɪn)
pick up
trip (trɪp)

They walked for six hours. Then they stopped for a rest. They all ate some of the food. Then there was less for the servant to carry. The servant's bundle grew smaller and lighter each day. By the end of the trip, the clever servant had nothing to carry.

---

then〔ðɛn〕
rest〔rɛst〕
less〔lɛs〕
grow〔gro〕
end〔ɛnd〕

2. The Clever Servant
聰明的僕人

中文翻譯

Here's an old story. A wealthy man wanted to make a journey to a faraway town. He was a businessman. He wanted to take products to sell. He also planned to take gold to buy things with. He decided to take ten servants with him. They would carry the goods to sell and the food to eat on the journey.

有個古老的故事是這樣說的。一個有錢人想到遙遠的城鎮去旅行。他是個商人。他想把產品帶去賣。他還計畫要帶金子去買東西。他決定帶十個僕人和他一起去。他們將帶著要出售的貨物，以及旅途上要吃的食物。

He was a kindhearted man. He said to one of his servants, "You are the shortest, the thinnest and the weakest of all my servants. You cannot carry a heavy bundle. You must choose the lightest bundle to carry."

富人是個好心人。他對其中一個僕人說：「你是所有僕人中最矮小，也最瘦弱的。你搬不動沉重的包裏。你必須選最輕的包袱來拿。」

** ———————————————

clever〔'klɛvɚ〕*adj.* 聰明的　servant〔'sɝvənt〕*n.* 僕人
wealthy〔'wɛlθɪ〕*adj.* 有錢的　journey〔'dʒɝnɪ〕*n.* 旅程
faraway〔'fɑrə'we〕*adj.* 遙遠的　carry〔'kærɪ〕*v.* 攜帶；搬運
goods〔gʊdz〕*n. pl.* 貨物　kindhearted〔'kaɪnd'hɑrtɪd〕*adj.* 好心的
thin〔θɪn〕*adj.* 瘦的　weak〔wik〕*adj.* 虛弱的
heavy〔'hɛvɪ〕*adj.* 沉重的　bundle〔'bʌndḷ〕*n.* 包裹；包袱

The servant thanked his master. He pointed to the largest bundle. This was the fruit and bread to eat on the journey.

這名僕人向主人道了謝。然後指著最大的包裹。這個包裹是裝旅程中要吃的水果和麵包。

"You are foolish," said his master. "That is the biggest and heaviest bundle." But the servant picked up the bundle cheerfully and the trip began. They walked for six hours. Then they stopped for a rest. They all ate some of the food. Then there was less for the servant to carry. The servant's bundle grew smaller and lighter each day. By the end of the trip, the clever servant had nothing to carry.

「你眞傻，」主人說。「那是最大、最重的擔子。」但僕人卻愉快地拿起那個包裹，開始了旅程。他們走了六個鐘頭。然後就停下來休息。所有的人都吃了一些食物。所以那個僕人要拿的東西就變少了。僕人的包裹一天天地減少、減輕。在旅程結束時，聰明的僕人已經沒有東西要拿了。

** ——————————

master〔ˈmæstɚ〕*n.* 主人　***point to*** 指著
bread〔brɛd〕*n.* 麵包　foolish〔ˈfulɪʃ〕*adj.* 愚蠢的
pick up 拿起　cheerfully〔ˈtʃɪrfəlɪ〕*adv.* 愉快地
trip〔trɪp〕*n.* 旅程　rest〔rɛst〕*n.* 休息
grow〔gro〕*v.* 變得　by〔baɪ〕*prep.* 到了
end〔ɛnd〕*n.* 結束

3. Polly's Dream

Polly was a farmer's daughter. She helped her mom do chores every day.

---

dream〔drim〕

farmer〔ˈfɑrmɚ〕

daughter〔ˈdɔtɚ〕

mom〔mɑm〕

chores〔tʃorz〕

One day her mom gave her a pail of milk.

"You are a good girl," said her mom.

"Take this bucket of milk to the village and sell it. You may keep every penny."

---

pail〔pel〕	milk〔mɪlk〕
bucket〔'bʌkɪt〕	village〔'vɪlɪdʒ〕
sell〔sɛl〕	penny〔'pɛnɪ〕

Polly was very pleased. "Oh, thank you so much, Mother," she said. She put the pail of milk on top of her head and started for the village. On the way she began thinking.

This is what she thought:

---

pleased (plizd) | ***on top of***
start for | ***on the way***
begin (bɪ'gɪn)

I will sell this milk. I will certainly get a lot of money for it. With this money, I will buy eggs. I hope to get two hundred eggs.

I will put those eggs under hens. Certainly at least one hundred and fifty of them will hatch. Then I can sell these chickens when they grow up. Then I will be rich.

---

certainly ('sɜtn̩lɪ)
hundred ('hʌndrəd)
at least
chicken ('tʃɪkən)
rich (rɪtʃ)
hope (hop)
hen (hɛn)
hatch (hætʃ)
grow up

With all the money, I will buy a new dress. I will look so beautiful in this new dress that every young man will want to marry me. I will toss my head and refuse them all.

---

dress [drɛs]
beautiful ['bjutəfəl]
young [jʌŋ]
marry ['mærɪ]
toss [tɔs]
toss *one's* ***head***
refuse [rɪ'fjuz]

So she tossed her head quickly.

Just then, the bucket came down and the milk spilled out. Poor girl! That was the end of her fine dream.

---

quickly〔ˈkwɪklɪ〕

then〔ðɛn〕

spill〔spɪl〕

end〔ɛnd〕

just〔dʒʌst〕

come down

poor〔pʊr〕

fine〔faɪn〕

3. Polly's Dream
波莉之夢

中文翻譯

Polly was a farmer's daughter. She helped her mom do chores every day.

波莉是一個農夫的女兒。她每天幫媽媽做家事。

One day her mom gave her a pail of milk. "You are a good girl," said her mom. "Take this bucket of milk to the village and sell it. You may keep every penny." Polly was very pleased. "Oh, thank you so much, Mother," she said. She put the pail of milk on top of her head and started for the village. On the way she began thinking.

有一天，她媽媽給她一桶牛奶。「妳是個乖女孩，」媽媽說。「把這桶牛奶帶到村裏去賣。妳可以把所有的錢都留著。」波莉聽了非常高興。「哦，媽媽，非常感謝妳！」她說。她頭上頂著那桶牛奶，出發往村裡去。在路上，她開始邊走邊想。

This is what she thought:

她是這樣想的：

**

dream〔drim〕*n.* 夢　daughter〔ˈdɔtɚ〕*n.* 女兒
mom〔mɑm〕*n.* 媽媽　chores〔tʃorz〕*n. pl.* 家事
pail〔pel〕*n.* 桶子　milk〔mɪlk〕*n.* 牛奶　bucket〔ˈbʌkɪt〕*n.* 一桶
village〔ˈvɪlɪdʒ〕*n.* 村莊　sell〔sɛl〕*v.* 賣　keep〔kip〕*v.* 保有
penny〔ˈpɛnɪ〕*n.* 一分錢；金錢　pleased〔plizd〕*adj.* 高興的
on top of 在…的上面　***start for*** 動身前往　***on the way*** 在路上

I will sell this milk. I will certainly get a lot of money for it. With this money, I will buy eggs. I hope to get two hundred eggs. I will put those eggs under hens. Certainly at least one hundred and fifty of them will hatch. Then I can sell these chickens when they grow up. Then I will be rich. With all the money, I will buy a new dress. I will look so beautiful in this new dress that every young man will want to marry me. I will toss my head and refuse them all.

我會賣掉這桶牛奶。我一定可以賣得一筆好價錢。我會用這筆錢來買蛋。我希望可以買到兩百個蛋。我會把蛋拿給母雞孵，其中至少有一百五十個蛋一定會孵出小雞來。小雞長大後，就把牠們賣掉，然後我會很有錢。用這些錢，我可以買一件新衣服。穿上新衣服，我會變得很美麗。所有的年輕人都會想和我結婚。而我會甩甩頭，拒絕所有人。

So she tossed her head quickly.

然後她很快地甩甩頭。

Just then, the bucket came down and the milk spilled out. Poor girl! That was the end of her fine dream.

就在那時候，桶子掉了下來，牛奶灑了出去。可憐的女孩！她的好夢就這樣結束了。

** ——————————

certainly〔ˈsɝtn̩lɪ〕*adv.* 一定　hundred〔ˈhʌndrəd〕*adj.* 一百的
hen〔hɛn〕*n.* 母雞　***at least*** 至少
hatch〔hætʃ〕*v.* 孵化　***grow up*** 長大
dress〔drɛs〕*n.* 服裝　beautiful〔ˈbjutəfəl〕*adj.* 美麗的
marry〔ˈmærɪ〕*v.* 結婚；娶　toss〔tɔs〕*v.* 甩；揮動
toss** one's **head （尤指輕蔑或不耐煩地）把頭一甩
refuse〔rɪˈfjuz〕*v.* 拒絕　just〔dʒʌst〕*adv.* 正好；恰好
then〔ðɛn〕*adv.* 那時　***come down*** 掉下來　spill〔spɪl〕*v.* 灑出
poor〔pur〕*adj.* 可憐的　fine〔faɪn〕*adj.* 美好的

4. The Donkey in the Lion's Skin

Once a donkey found a lion's skin near the forest. He put it on, but, to tell the truth, it didn't suit him well.

---

donkey〔ˈdɑŋkɪ〕
skin〔skɪn〕
near〔nɪr〕
put on
to tell the truth
well〔wɛl〕
lion〔ˈlaɪən〕
once〔wʌns〕
forest〔ˈfɔrɪst〕
truth〔truθ〕
suit〔sut〕

When he walked around the area, he discovered that all the silly animals were frightened of him because they thought he was a lion.

---

around [əˈraʊnd]　　area [ˈɛrɪə]
discover [dɪˈskʌvɚ]　　silly [ˈsɪlɪ]
frightened [ˈfraɪtn̩d]

As soon as they saw him, they fled in terror. So he amused himself by tricking them often.

"Now I am the king of all beasts. I am a fierce lion. Everyone fears me," he said.

---

as soon as
terror〔ˈtɛrɚ〕
amuse〔əˈmjuz〕
trick〔trɪk〕
beast〔bist〕
fear〔fɪr〕
flee〔fli〕
in terror
amuse *oneself*
king〔kɪŋ〕
fierce〔fɪrs〕

By chance he met a fox, and he shouted loudly to surprise him. "Excuse me, but what are you doing?" asked the clever fox calmly.

---

by chance

fox〔fɑks〕

loudly〔'laudlɪ〕

Excuse me.

calmly〔'kɑmlɪ〕

meet〔mit〕

shout〔ʃaut〕

surprise〔sə'praɪz〕

clever〔'klɛvɚ〕

"I'm a lion; can't you hear my roar?" the simple donkey cried out.

"No," said the fox with a thin smile, "you are braying, not roaring. You must be a donkey."

"How do you know I am a donkey?" said the foolish animal.

---

roar 〔 ror 〕	simple 〔'sɪmpl̩ 〕
cry out	thin 〔 θɪn 〕
smile 〔 smaɪl 〕	bray 〔 bre 〕
foolish 〔'fulɪʃ 〕	animal 〔'ænəml̩ 〕

"If you kept silent, I would be afraid of your appearance. But I know your sound very well." So saying, he laughed and went away.

---

keep [kip]	silent [ˈsaɪlənt]
afraid [əˈfred]	appearance [əˈpɪrəns]
sound [saʊnd]	laugh [læf]

4. The Donkey in the Lion's Skin
披著獅皮的驢

中文翻譯

Once a donkey found a lion's skin near the forest. He put it on, but, to tell the truth, it didn't suit him well.

從前，有一隻驢子在森林附近，發現了一張獅皮。牠把獅皮穿上，但是，老實說，獅皮根本不適合牠。

When he walked around the area, he discovered that all the silly animals were frightened of him because they thought he was a lion. As soon as they saw him, they fled in terror. So he amused himself by tricking them often.

當牠在那一帶到處走動時，牠發現那些愚蠢的動物都很怕牠，因爲牠們認爲牠是隻獅子。動物們一看到牠，都被嚇跑了。所以牠就常以欺騙動物爲樂。

"Now I am the king of all beasts. I am a fierce lion. Everyone fears me," he said.

「現在，我是萬獸之王。我是一隻兇猛的獅子。每個人都怕我」，牠說。

**

donkey〔'dɑŋkɪ〕*n.* 驢子　forest〔'fɔrɪst〕*n.* 森林　***put on*** 穿上
to tell the truth 老實說　suit〔sut〕*v.* 適合　area〔'ɛrɪə〕*n.* 區域
discover〔dɪ'skʌvɚ〕*v.* 發現　silly〔'sɪlɪ〕*adj.* 愚蠢的
frightened〔'fraɪtṇd〕*adj.* 害怕的　***as soon as*** 一…就
flee〔fli〕*v.* 逃跑　***in terror*** 恐懼地
amuse *oneself* 消遣；取樂；自娛　trick〔trɪk〕*v.* 欺騙
beast〔bist〕*n.* 野獸　fierce〔fɪrs〕*adj.* 兇猛的

By chance he met a fox, and he shouted loudly to surprise him. "Excuse me, but what are you doing?" asked the clever fox calmly.

偶然地，牠遇到一隻狐狸，牠就大聲吼叫要嚇唬牠。「抱歉，但是你在做什麼？」聰明的狐狸鎮靜地問。

"I'm a lion; can't you hear my roar?" the simple donkey cried out. "No," said the fox with a thin smile, "you are braying, not roaring. You must be a donkey."

「我是隻獅子；你沒聽見我的吼叫聲嗎？」愚蠢的驢子大叫。「不，」狐狸帶著淺笑說：「那是驢叫，不是獅吼。你一定是隻驢子。」

"How do you know I am a donkey?" said the foolish animal.

「你怎麼知道我是驢子？」愚蠢的驢子說。

"If you kept silent, I would be afraid of your appearance. But I know your sound very well." So saying, he laughed and went away.

「如果你保持沉默，我就會因爲你的外表而害怕。但是我對你的聲音清楚得很。」說完這些話後，狐狸笑著走開。

**

by chance 偶然地 meet〔mit〕*v.* 遇見 shout〔ʃaʊt〕*v.* 吼叫
loudly〔ˈlaʊdlɪ〕*adv.* 大聲地 surprise〔səˈpraɪz〕*v.* 使驚訝
Excuse me. 抱歉。 clever〔ˈklɛvɚ〕*adj.* 聰明的
fox〔fɑks〕*n.* 狐狸 calmly〔ˈkɑmlɪ〕*adv.* 鎮靜地
roar〔ror〕*n.* 吼叫聲 *v.* 吼叫 simple〔ˈsɪmpl̩〕*adj.* 愚蠢的
cry out 叫喊 ***with a thin smile*** 淺淺地微笑
bray〔bre〕*v.*（驢）叫 foolish〔ˈfulɪʃ〕*adj.* 愚蠢的
keep〔kip〕*v.* 保持 silent〔ˈsaɪlənt〕*adj.* 沉默的
appearance〔əˈpɪrəns〕*n.* 外表 sound〔saʊnd〕*n.* 聲音
So saying,… 說完這些話後（＝*After saying so,…*）

5. *In a Train Car*

Nick went with his father to see his grandmother.

On the train Nick put his head out of the window every minute. His father said, "Nick, sit still! Don't put your head out of the window!" But Nick went on putting his head out of the window.

---

car〔 kɑr 〕
grandmother〔ˈgrænˌmʌðɚ〕
put A ***out of*** B
window〔ˈwɪndo〕
minute〔ˈmɪnɪt〕
still〔 stɪl 〕
go on

His father took Nick's cap quietly, hid it behind his back and said, "You see, your cap has been blown away." Nick was afraid. He began to cry. He wanted to have his cap back.

---

cap 〔 kæp 〕
quietly 〔 'kwaɪətlɪ 〕
hide 〔 haɪd 〕
behind 〔 bɪ'haɪnd 〕
blow 〔 blo 〕
afraid 〔 ə'fred 〕
begin 〔 bɪ'gɪn 〕

His father said, "Well, whistle once! Perhaps, your cap will come back." Nick went up to the window and whistled. Nick's father quickly put the cap on Nick's head.

---

whistle〔'hwɪsḷ〕

once〔wʌns〕

perhaps〔pɚ'hæps〕

go up to

quickly〔'kwɪklɪ〕

"Oh! That was wonderful!" Nick laughed. He was pleased. He took his

father's cap quickly and threw it out of the window. "Now it's your turn to whistle, Dad!" he said gaily.

---

wonderful〔'wʌndɚfəl〕 laugh〔læf〕
pleased〔plizd〕 throw〔θro〕
turn〔tɝn〕 gaily〔'gelɪ〕

5. In a Train Car
車 廂 中

中文翻譯

Nick went with his father to see his grandmother.

尼克和父親一起去探望祖母。

On the train Nick put his head out of the window every minute. His father said, "Nick, sit still! Don't put your head out of the window!" But Nick went on putting his head out of the window.

在火車上，尼克不斷把頭伸出窗外。他的父親說：「尼克，坐好！不要把頭伸出窗外！」但是尼克還是繼續把頭伸出窗外。

His father took Nick's cap quietly, hid it behind his back and said, "You see, your cap has been blown away." Nick was afraid. He began to cry. He wanted to have his cap back.

尼克的父親悄悄拿走他的帽子，藏在背後，然後說：「你看吧，你的帽子被吹走了。」尼克很害怕。他開始哭。他想拿回他的帽子。

**

car〔 kɑr 〕*n.* 車廂　grandmother〔ˈgræn,mʌðɚ〕*n.*（外）祖母
put A ***out of*** B 把 A 伸出 B 之外　minute〔ˈmɪnɪt〕*n.* 分鐘
still〔 stɪl 〕*adj.* 不動的　***sit still*** 坐著不動　***go on*** 繼續
cap〔 kæp 〕*n.*（無邊的）帽子　quietly〔ˈkwaɪətlɪ〕*adv.* 悄悄地
hide〔 haɪd 〕*v.* 藏匿【過去式爲 hid〔 hɪd 〕】
behind〔 bɪˈhaɪnd 〕*prep.* 在…後面　blow〔 blo 〕*v.* 吹
afraid〔 əˈfred 〕*adj.* 害怕的

His father said, "Well, whistle once! Perhaps, your cap will come back." Nick went up to the window and whistled. Nick's father quickly put the cap on Nick's head.

他的父親說：「嗯，吹一聲口哨！或許你的帽子就會回來。」尼克走到窗邊吹口哨。尼克的父親很快地把帽子放到他頭上。

"Oh! That was wonderful!" Nick laughed. He was pleased. He took his father's cap quickly and threw it out of the window. "Now it's your turn to whistle, Dad!" he said gaily.

「喔！太棒了！」尼克笑著說。他很高興。他快速拿起父親的帽子，然後把它扔出窗外。「現在換你吹口哨了，爹地！」他愉快地說。

** ————————————

whistle〔'hwɪsḷ〕*v.* 吹口哨
once〔wʌns〕*adv.* 一次
perhaps〔pɚ'hæps〕*adv.* 或許
go up to 走近
wonderful〔'wʌndɚfəl〕*adj.* 很棒的
laugh〔læf〕*v.* 笑
pleased〔plizd〕*adj.* 高興的
turn〔tɝn〕*n.* 輪流順序
it's your turn 輪到你了　gaily〔'gelɪ〕*adv.* 愉快地

6. I Am Not a Bear

Old Mr. White loved shooting bears, but his eyes kept getting worse. Several times he almost shot people instead of bears, so his friends were always very careful when they went out hunting with him.

---

bear〔 bɛr 〕
eye〔 aɪ 〕
worse〔 wɝs 〕
time〔 taɪm 〕
instead of
hunt〔 hʌnt 〕

shoot〔 ʃut 〕
keep〔 kip 〕
several〔ˈsɛvərəl 〕
almost〔ˈɔl,most 〕
careful〔ˈkɛrfəl 〕

One day a friend of his wanted to play a joke. So he got a big piece of paper and wrote on it in very big letters "I AM NOT A BEAR". Then he tied it to his back and went off. Everyone who saw it laughed a lot.

---

one day joke〔dʒok〕
play a joke piece〔pis〕
paper〔ˈpepɚ〕 letter〔ˈlɛtɚ〕
tie〔taɪ〕 ***go off***
laugh〔læf〕 ***a lot***

But the sign did not save him.

After a few minutes, Mr. White shot at him and knocked his hat off.

---

sign 〔 saɪn 〕 save 〔 sev 〕

minute 〔ˈmɪnɪt 〕 knock 〔 nɑk 〕

hat 〔 hæt 〕 ***knock ~ off***

The young man was upset and angry. "Didn't you see this piece of paper?" he shouted to Mr. White. "I sure did," said Mr. White. Then he went closer, looked carefully at the paper and said, "Oh, I am so sorry. I did not see the word NOT."

---

upset〔ʌp'sɛt〕
shout〔ʃaʊt〕
close〔klos〕
carefully〔'kɛrfəlɪ〕
angry〔'æŋgrɪ〕
sure〔ʃʊr〕

6. I Am Not a Bear

我不是熊

中文翻譯

Old Mr. White loved shooting bears, but his eyes kept getting worse. Several times he almost shot people instead of bears, so his friends were always very careful when they went out hunting with him.

老懷特先生喜歡獵熊，但是他的視力一直變差。好幾次，都差點射中人，而不是熊，所以他的朋友跟他一起去打獵時，總是非常小心。

One day a friend of his wanted to play a joke. So he got a big piece of paper and wrote on it in very big letters "I AM NOT A BEAR". Then he tied it to his back and went off. Everyone who saw it laughed a lot.

一天，他的一位朋友想開個玩笑。於是他拿了一大張紙，並寫上「我不是熊」幾個大字。接著他把那張紙綁在背上，然後就走開。每個人看到都哈哈大笑。

** ———

shoot (ʃut) *v.* 射中；打獵【過去式為 shot (ʃɑt)】
keep (kip) *v.* 一直　get (gɛt) *v.* 變得　worse (wɝs) *adj.* 更糟的
several (ˈsɛvərəl) *adj.* 幾個的　time (taɪm) *n.* 次
almost (ˈɔlˌmost) *adv.* 差一點　***instead of*** 而不是
hunt (hʌnt) *v.* 打獵　joke (dʒok) *n.* 玩笑
play a joke (on sb.) 跟（某人）開玩笑
piece (pis) *n.* 張；片　letter (ˈlɛtɚ) *n.* 文字；字母
tie (taɪ) *v.* 繫；綁　***go off*** 離開　laugh (læf) *v.* 笑

But the sign did not save him. After a few minutes, Mr. White shot at him and knocked his hat off.

但是這張告示卻救不了他。幾分鐘後，懷特先生射中他，而且還把他的帽子擊落。

The young man was upset and angry. "Didn't you see this piece of paper?" he shouted to Mr. White. "I sure did," said Mr. White. Then he went closer, looked carefully at the paper and said, "Oh, I am so sorry. I did not see the word NOT."

這位年輕人很生氣。「你沒看到這張紙嗎？」他對懷特先生大叫。「我當然有看到，」懷特先生說。然後他走近一點，仔細地看那張紙，他說：「喔，很抱歉。我沒有看見『不』這個字。」

**

sign〔saɪn〕*n.* 告示
save〔sev〕*v.* 拯救　***knock～off*** 將～擊落
hat〔hæt〕*n.* 帽子　upset〔ʌp'sɛt〕*adj.* 不高興的
angry〔'æŋgrɪ〕*adj.* 生氣的　piece〔pis〕*n.*（一）張
paper〔'pepɚ〕*n.* 紙　shout〔ʃaʊt〕*v.* 大叫
sure〔ʃur〕*adv.* 當然；確實　close〔klos〕*adv.* 接近地

7. *It's a Boy or a Girl*

Many kids in the U.S.A. today are wearing the same clothes, and many of them have long hair, so it's not often easy to tell whether they are male or female.

---

kid〔kɪd〕
wear〔wɛr〕
clothes〔kloðz〕
tell〔tɛl〕
male〔mel〕
the U.S.A.
same〔sem〕
hair〔hɛr〕
whether〔ˈhwɛðɚ〕
female〔ˈfimel〕

For example, one day an old lady went for a walk near a lake, and when she was tired she sat down on a bench. A teenager was standing on the other side of the lake.

"Pardon me," the old lady said to the person next to her on the bench. "Do you see that kid with the red pants and long hair? Is that a boy or a girl?"

---

lady ['ledɪ]
tired [taɪrd]
teenager ['tin,edʒɚ]
pardon ['pɑrdn̩]
next [nɛkst]
pants [pænts]

lake [lek]
bench [bɛntʃ]
side [saɪd]
Pardon me.
next to

"It's a girl," said her neighbor, "She's my daughter."

"Oh!" the old lady said in a hurry. "I'm sorry, but I didn't know that you were her mother."

"I'm not," said the other person. "I'm her dad."

---

neighbor〔'nebɚ〕　daughter〔'dɔtɚ〕
hurry〔'hɝɪ〕　***in a hurry***
dad〔dæd〕

7. It's a Boy or a Girl
男孩還是女孩

中文翻譯

Many kids in the U.S.A. today are wearing the same clothes, and many of them have long hair, so it's not often easy to tell whether they are male or female.

美國現在有許多孩子穿著相同的衣服，而且其中有許多人留長頭髮，所以要分辨他們是男的還是女的，常常不太容易。

For example, one day an old lady went for a walk near a lake, and when she was tired she sat down on a bench. A teenager was standing on the other side of the lake.

舉例來說，有一天，一位老婦人到湖的附近散步，後來她走累了，就坐在一張長椅上。有個青少年正好站在湖的另一邊。

** ——————————————

kid〔kɪd〕*n.* 小孩　***the U.S.A.*** 美國（= *the United States of America*）
wear〔wɛr〕*v.* 穿；戴　same〔sem〕*adj.* 相同的
clothes〔kloðz〕*n. pl.* 衣服　hair〔hɛr〕*n.* 頭髮　tell〔tɛl〕*v.* 分辨
whether A ***or*** B 是 A 還是 B　male〔mel〕*adj.* 男的
female〔ˈfimel〕*adj.* 女的　***for example*** 舉例來說　***one day*** 有一天
lady〔ˈledɪ〕*n.* 女士　***go for a walk*** 去散步　lake〔lek〕*n.* 湖
tired〔taɪrd〕*adj.* 累的　bench〔bɛntʃ〕*n.* 長椅
teenager〔ˈtin,edʒɚ〕*n.* 青少年　side〔saɪd〕*n.* 邊

"Pardon me," the old lady said to the person next to her on the bench. "Do you see that kid with the red pants and long hair? Is that a boy or a girl?"

「恕我冒昧，」老婦人對坐在旁邊的人說。「你有看到那個穿著紅褲子，留長頭髮的孩子嗎？他是男孩還是女孩啊？」

"It's a girl," said her neighbor, "She's my daughter."

「她是個女孩，」坐在旁邊的人說。「她是我女兒。」

"Oh!" the old lady said in a hurry. "I'm sorry, but I didn't know that you were her mother."

「噢！」老婦人很快地說。「很抱歉，我不知道妳是她的母親。」

"I'm not," said the other person. "I'm her dad."

「我不是，」那人說。「我是她的父親。」

** ——————————————

Pardon me. 對不起；恕我冒昧。
next to 在…隔壁
pants [pænts] *n. pl.* 褲子
neighbor [ˈnebɚ] *n.* 鄰座的人
daughter [ˈdɔtɚ] *n.* 女兒
in a hurry 急忙地　dad [dæd] *n.* 爸爸

8. The Farmer, His Horse, and His Son

Once upon a time there was an old farmer, who had a very old, but still beautiful horse. He decided to go to the market with his young son, to sell the horse before it died.

They both walked, because the farmer did not want to tire out the horse.

---

horse [hɔrs]
beautiful [ˈbjutəfəl]
market [ˈmɑrkɪt]
sell [sɛl]
tire out
once upon a time
decide [dɪˈsaɪd]
young [jʌŋ]
die [daɪ]

They met two women on the way who said, "Why aren't you riding, farmer? You have a nice horse. It's a long way to

the market." The farmer knew that this was true, so he hopped on the horse, while his son walked.

---

meet 〔 mit 〕

ride 〔 raɪd 〕

true 〔 tru 〕

while 〔 hwaɪl 〕

on the way

nice 〔 naɪs 〕

hop 〔 hɑp 〕

Then they met two old men who asked, "What are you doing there, farmer? Your boy is tired. You are cruel." So the farmer got off, and let his son ride instead.

---

then [ðɛn]
tired [taɪrd]
cruel [ˈkruəl]
get off
let [lɛt]
instead [ɪnˈstɛd]

Next, three young men stopped them. One said, "Why are you walking, farmer? Ride your horse. It's too hot today for an old guy like you to walk." So the farmer got up again, and rode together with his son.

---

next [nɛkst]	stop [stɑp]
too…to~	guy [gaɪ]
get up	together [təˈgɛðɚ]

A little while later, a young lady passed them. "Why aren't you walking?" she asked. "It isn't far to the market. Give your beautiful old horse a rest."

So the farmer, and his son, got off once more.

The lesson they learned is: you cannot please all people all the time.

---

a little	while [hwaɪl]
later ['letɚ]	pass [pæs]
far [fɑr]	rest [rɛst]
once more	lesson ['lɛsn̩]
please [pliz]	***all the time***

8. The Farmer, His Horse, and His Son
農夫、馬和他的兒子

中文翻譯

Once upon a time there was an old farmer, who had a very old, but still beautiful horse. He decided to go to the market with his young son, to sell the horse before it died. They both walked, because the farmer did not want to tire out the horse.

從前有位老農夫，他有一匹很老，但是仍然很漂亮的馬。他決定要在那匹馬死前，和年輕的兒子一起把牠帶到市場賣掉。他們兩個都用走的，因爲農夫不想累壞那匹馬。

They met two women on the way who said, "Why aren't you riding, farmer? You have a nice horse. It's a long way to the market." The farmer knew that this was true, so he hopped on the horse, while his son walked.

他們在路上碰到兩個婦人，她們說：「農夫，你爲什麼不騎馬？你有一匹好馬。到市場的路途還很遙遠。」農夫知道這是事實，所以他跳上馬，讓兒子用走的。

** ——————————

farmer〔ˈfɑrmɚ〕*n.* 農夫　horse〔hɔrs〕*n.* 馬　son〔sʌn〕*n.* 兒子
once upon a time 從前　beautiful〔ˈbjutəfəl〕*adj.* 漂亮的
decide〔dɪˈsaɪd〕*v.* 決定　market〔ˈmɑrkɪt〕*n.* 市場
young〔jʌŋ〕*adj.* 年輕的　sell〔sɛl〕*v.* 賣　die〔daɪ〕*v.* 死
tire out 使筋疲力竭　meet〔mit〕*v.* 遇見　***on the way*** 在途中
ride〔raɪd〕*v.* 騎馬　nice〔naɪs〕*adj.* 好的　true〔tru〕*adj.* 眞的
hop on 跳上　while〔hwaɪl〕*conj.* 然而

Then they met two old men who asked, "What are you doing there, farmer? Your boy is tired. You are cruel." So the farmer got off, and let his son ride instead.

後來他們遇到兩個老人，他們說：「農夫，你在上面做什麼？你的兒子很累。你眞殘忍。」因此，農夫就下馬來，換他兒子騎馬。

Next, three young men stopped them. One said, "Why are you walking, farmer? Ride your horse. It's too hot today for an old guy like you to walk." So the farmer got up again, and rode together with his son.

接著，有三個年輕人叫住他們。其中一個說：「農夫，你幹嘛走路？快上馬。對你這樣的老人來說，今天太熱了，不適合走路。」所以農夫又再次上馬，和兒子一起騎馬。

**

then [ðɛn] *adv.* 後來　tired [taɪrd] *adj.* 疲倦的
cruel ['kruəl] *adj.* 殘忍的　***get off*** 下來
let [lɛt] *v.* 讓　instead [ɪn'stɛd] *adv.* 作爲代替
next [nɛkst] *adv.* 接著　stop [stap] *v.* 使停止
too…to～ 太…以致於不～　guy [gaɪ] *n.* (男) 人
like [laɪk] *prep.* 像　***together with*** 和～一起

A little while later, a young lady passed them. "Why aren't you walking?" she asked. "It isn't far to the market. Give your beautiful old horse a rest."

過了不久，一位年輕女子經過他們身邊。「你們爲什麼不用走的？」她問。「到市場並不遠。讓你那匹漂亮的老馬休息一下吧。」

So the farmer, and his son, got off once more.

於是農夫和他兒子又再次下馬。

The lesson they learned is: you cannot please all people all the time.

他們所學到的教訓就是：你始終無法取悅所有人。

** ——————————————

while〔hwaɪl〕*n.*（短暫的）時間
a little while 不久　later〔ˈletɚ〕*adv.* 之後
pass〔pæs〕*v.* 經過　far〔fɑr〕*adj.* 遙遠的
rest〔rɛst〕*n.* 休息　***once more*** 再一次
lesson〔ˈlɛsn̩〕*n.* 教訓　learn〔lɝn〕*v.* 學習
please〔pliz〕*v.* 取悅　***all the time*** 始終；經常

9. A Slip of the Tongue

Mr. and Mrs. Parker got married twenty-five years ago, and they have lived in the same house since then.

---

slip〔slɪp〕

a slip of the tongue

get married

same〔sem〕

then〔ðɛn〕

tongue〔tʌŋ〕

married〔ˈmærɪd〕

ago〔əˈgo〕

since〔sɪns〕

Mr. Parker goes to work at seven-thirty a.m. every day, and he gets home at six-thirty p.m. every evening, from Monday to Friday.

---

a.m. [ˈeˈɛm]	get [gɛt]
p.m. [ˈpiˈɛm]	evening [ˈivnɪŋ]
Monday [ˈmʌnde]	Friday [ˈfraɪde]

There are many houses on their street, and most of the residents are nice. But the old man in the house opposite Mr. and Mrs. Parker died, and after a few weeks a young couple came to live in it.

---

street (strit)
nice (naɪs)
die (daɪ)
couple (′kʌpl̩)
resident (′rɛzədənt)
opposite (′ɑpəzɪt)
young (jʌŋ)

Mrs. Parker observed them for a few days from her window and then she said to her husband, “Fred, the man in that house across from ours always kisses his wife when he leaves for work and he kisses her again when he returns home at night. Why don’t you do that, too?”

“Well,” Mr. Parker replied, “I don’t know her well enough yet.”

---

observe 〔əbˈzɝv〕 window 〔ˈwɪndo〕
then 〔ðɛn〕 husband 〔ˈhʌzbənd〕
wife 〔waɪf〕 leave 〔liv〕
return 〔rɪˈtɝn〕 reply 〔rɪˈplaɪ〕
enough 〔əˈnʌf〕 yet 〔jɛt〕

9. A Slip of the Tongue

說溜了嘴

中文翻譯

Mr. and Mrs. Parker got married twenty-five years ago, and they have lived in the same house since then. Mr. Parker goes to work at seven-thirty a.m. every day, and he gets home at six-thirty p.m. every evening, from Monday to Friday.

派克夫婦結婚二十五年了，而且從結婚那時候起，他們就一直住在同一棟房子裡。星期一到星期五，派克先生每天早上都七點半去上班，然後每天晚上六點半到家。

There are many houses on their street, and most of the residents are nice. But the old man in the house opposite Mr. and Mrs. Parker died, and after a few weeks a young couple came to live in it.

在他們住的那條街上，有很多戶人家，而且大多數的居民都很好。但是住在派克夫婦對面那棟房子的老人去世了，而且幾個星期後，一對年輕夫婦搬了進去。

**

slip〔slɪp〕*n.* 失言　tongue〔tʌŋ〕*n.* 舌頭
a slip of the tongue 失言；說溜了嘴　married〔ˈmærɪd〕*adj.* 結婚的
get married 結婚　ago〔əˈgo〕*adv.* …以前
same〔sem〕*adj.* 相同的　since〔sɪns〕*prep.* 自…以來
then〔ðɛn〕*adv.* 那時　***since then*** 從那時起
a.m.〔ˈeˈɛm〕*adv.* 早上　get〔gɛt〕*v.* 到達　p.m.〔ˈpiˈɛm〕*adv.* 下午
resident〔ˈrɛzədənt〕*n.* 居民　opposite〔ˈɑpəzɪt〕*prep.* 在…對面
die〔daɪ〕*v.* 死　couple〔ˈkʌpl̩〕*n.* 夫妻

Mrs. Parker observed them for a few days from her window and then she said to her husband, "Fred, the man in that house across from ours always kisses his wife when he leaves for work and he kisses her again when he returns home at night. Why don't you do that, too?"

派克太太從窗戶觀察他們幾天之後，便對她的丈夫說：「佛瑞德，住在我們對面那棟房子的男人，每天早上出門上班時，總是會親吻他的妻子，晚上回家時，又再度親吻她。你為什麼不也那樣做呢？」

"Well," Mr. Parker replied, "I don't know her well enough yet."

「嗯，」派克先生回答：「我跟她還不夠熟。」

** ————————————————

observe〔əb'zɝv〕*v.* 觀察　window〔'wɪndo〕*n.* 窗戶
then〔ðɛn〕*adv.* 然後　husband〔'hʌzbənd〕*n.* 丈夫
across from 在…的對面　kiss〔kɪs〕*v.* 親吻
wife〔waɪf〕*n.* 妻子　leave〔liv〕*v.* 離開
return〔rɪ'tɝn〕*v.* 返回
well〔wɛl〕*interj.* 嗯　*adv.* 全然地；十分地
reply〔rɪ'plaɪ〕*v.* 回答
enough〔ə'nʌf〕*adv.* 足夠地；充分地
jet〔jɛt〕*adv.* 尚（未）

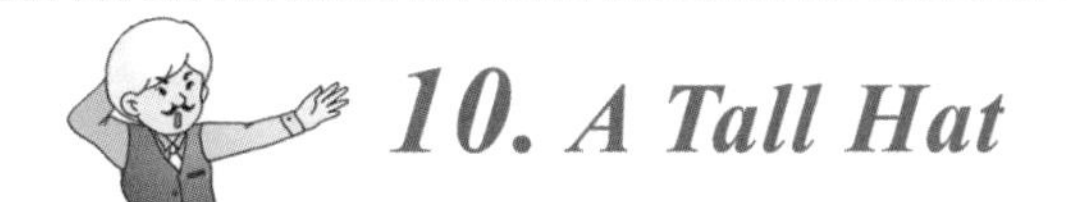

10. A Tall Hat

To flatter someone is called putting tall hats on his or her head.

---

tall ﹝tɔl﹞

tall hat

head ﹝hɛd﹞

put tall hat on *one's* ***head***

hat ﹝hæt﹞

flatter ﹝ˈflætɚ﹞

Once a little official was told to work in the capital city. Before he left, he visited his teacher, a big official, to say good-bye. The big official advised him:

"When you work in the capital city, you must be careful in everything that you do. Never offend other officials."

---

once〔wʌns〕
official〔ə'fɪʃəl〕
capital city
visit〔'vɪzɪt〕
careful〔'kɛrfəl〕
little〔'lɪtḷ〕
capital〔'kæpətḷ〕
leave〔liv〕
advise〔əd'vaɪz〕
offend〔ə'fɛnd〕

"Don't worry, I promise I won't," the clever official said.

"I have prepared 100 tall hats that will make everyone happy."

---

worry ['wɝɪ] promise ['prɑmɪs]

clever ['klɛvɚ] prepare [prɪ'pɛr]

His teacher became very angry. He said, “Men of learning shouldn’t do such things.”

---

become 〔 bɪ'kʌm 〕 angry 〔'æŋgrɪ 〕
learning 〔'lɝnɪŋ 〕 ***man of learning***
such 〔 sʌtʃ 〕

The little official replied, "But most people, except you, of course, like to have tall hats put on their heads."

"That's true," the big official smiled and nodded. "What you say is correct."

reply (rɪˈplaɪ)
except (ɪkˈsɛpt)
of course
true (tru)
smile (smaɪl)
nod (nɑd)
correct (kəˈrɛkt)

The clever official went home and told some of his friends, "Well, now I only have 99 tall hats, for I have given my first one away.

---

give away first〔fɝst〕

10. A Tall Hat
高帽子

中文翻譯

To flatter someone is called putting tall hats on his or her head.

奉承某人，就叫作給他或她戴高帽子。

Once a little official was told to work in the capital city. Before he left, he visited his teacher, a big official, to say good-bye. The big official advised him:

從前有位小官員，他被通知要去首都工作。在離開前，他去拜訪他的老師——一位大官，並向他辭行。那位大官建議他：

"When you work in the capital city, you must be careful in everything that you do. Never offend other officials."

「你在首都工作時，凡事都得小心。絕不能得罪其他官員。」

**

tall hat 高帽子；大禮帽
flatter [ˈflætɚ] *v.* 奉承；諂媚　head [hɛd] *n.* 頭
put tall hat on one's head 給某人戴高帽子；奉承某人
once [wʌns] *adv.* 從前　official [əˈfɪʃəl] *n.* 官員
capital [ˈkæpətl̩] *adj.* 首都的　leave [liv] *v.* 離開（過去式爲 left [lɛft]）
visit [ˈvɪzɪt] *v.* 拜訪　advise [ədˈvaɪz] *v.* 建議；勸告
careful [ˈkɛrfəl] *adj.* 小心的　offend [əˈfɛnd] *v.* 冒犯；得罪

"Don't worry, I promise I won't," the clever official said. "I have prepared 100 tall hats that will make everyone happy."

「別擔心，我保證我不會得罪他們，」這位聰明的官員說。「我已經準備好一百頂高帽子，會讓每個人都開心的。」

His teacher became very angry. He said, "Men of learning shouldn't do such things."

他的老師很生氣。他說：「學者不該做這樣的事。」

The little official replied, "But most people, except you, of course, like to have tall hats put on their heads."

小官員回答說：「但是大多數的人都喜歡把高帽子戴在頭上，當然，除了你之外。」

"That's true," the big official smiled and nodded. "What you say is correct."

「沒錯，」大官微笑著點頭說。「你說得很對。」

The clever official went home and told some of his friends, "Well, now I only have 99 tall hats, for I have given my first one away.

這位聰明的官員回家之後，告訴他的一些朋友說：「嗯，我現在只剩九十九頂高帽子，因爲我已經把第一頂送出去了。」

** ─────────────

promise〔ˈprɑmɪs〕*v.* 保證　clever〔ˈklɛvɚ〕*adj.* 聰明的
prepare〔prɪˈpɛr〕*v.* 準備　***man of learning*** 學者
reply〔rɪˈplaɪ〕*v.* 回答　except〔ɪkˈsɛpt〕*prep.* 除了…之外
nod〔nɑd〕*v.* 點頭　correct〔kəˈrɛkt〕*adj.* 正確的
for〔fɚ〕*prep.* 因爲　***give away*** 贈送；送掉

11. Interesting Words

Kathy keeps a record of new words and terms in English. She usually writes them in a small notebook.

---

interesting〔ˈɪntrɪstɪŋ〕
keep〔kip〕
term〔tɝm〕
notebook〔ˈnot,bʊk〕
word〔wɝd〕
record〔ˈrɛkɚd〕
usually〔ˈjuʒʊəlɪ〕

Then she often asks her

teacher about them.

"Mrs. Jones, these terms

are new to me. He's

blue today. What's the

matter? You're yellow?

A little white lie. She

has a green thumb.

Blue and yellow people

with green thumbs?

White lie? Could you

explain what they mean, please?

---

blue 〔 blu 〕

yellow 〔ˈjɛlo 〕

lie 〔 laɪ 〕

explain 〔 ɪkˈsplen 〕

matter 〔ˈmætɚ 〕

white 〔 hwaɪt 〕

thumb 〔 θʌm 〕

mean 〔 min 〕

Mrs. Jones replied, "Sure. In everyday English, Kathy, blue means sad. Yellow means afraid. A person with a green thumb grows plants very well. And a white lie is not a very bad thing."

---

reply 〔 rɪ'plaɪ 〕
everyday 〔'ɛvrɪ'de 〕
sad 〔 sæd 〕
afraid 〔 ə'fred 〕
grow 〔 gro 〕
plant 〔 plænt 〕

"I don't understand. Please give me an example."

"For example, I offer you some cake, but you don't like it. You don't say that. Instead, you say, 'No, thanks. I'm not hungry.' That's a white lie."

"Oh, I see. Thanks for the explanation."

---

understand〔ˌʌndɚˈstænd〕
example〔ɪgˈzæmpl̩〕 ***for example***
offer〔ˈɔfɚ〕 instead〔ɪnˈstɛd〕
hungry〔ˈhʌŋgrɪ〕 see〔si〕
explanation〔ˌɛkspləˈneʃən〕

11. Interesting Words
有趣的字

中文翻譯

Kathy keeps a record of new words and terms in English. She usually writes them in a small notebook. Then she often asks her teacher about them. "Mrs. Jones, these terms are new to me. He's blue today. What's the matter? You're yellow? A little white lie. She has a green thumb. Blue and yellow people with green thumbs? White lie? Could you explain what they mean, please?"

凱西記下了一些英文生字和詞語。她通常將它們寫在一本小筆記本上。然後，她常常會拿去問她的老師。「瓊斯太太，我第一次聽到這些詞語。他今天是藍色的。這是怎麼回事？你是黃色的？一個小小的白色謊言。她有根綠色的拇指。有著綠拇指的藍色及黃色的人？白色的謊言？可不可以請妳解釋一下它們的意思？」

** ——————————————

interesting〔ˈɪntrɪstɪŋ〕*adj.* 有趣的　　word〔wɝd〕*n.* 字
keep〔kip〕*v.* 記載　　record〔ˈrɛkɚd〕*n.* 記錄；記載
new〔nju〕*adj.* 第一次看到的　　term〔tɝm〕*n.* 詞語
usually〔ˈjuʒuəlɪ〕*adv.* 通常　　notebook〔ˈnot,buk〕*n.* 筆記本
blue〔blu〕*adj.* 藍色的；憂鬱的　　***What's the matter?*** 怎麼了？
yellow〔ˈjɛlo〕*adj.* 黃色的；膽小的　　white〔hwaɪt〕*adj.* 白色的；善意的
lie〔laɪ〕*n.* 謊言　　***white lie*** 善意的謊言
green〔grin〕*adj.* 綠色的　　thumb〔θʌm〕*n.* 拇指
green thumb 園藝的才能　　with〔wɪð〕*prep.* 有…的
explain〔ɪkˈsplen〕*v.* 解釋　　mean〔min〕*v.* 意思是

Mrs. Jones replied, "Sure. In everyday English, Kathy, blue means sad. Yellow means afraid. A person with a green thumb grows plants very well. And a white lie is not a very bad thing."

瓊斯太太回答說：「好的。凱西，在日常英語中，藍色意味著憂傷。黃色表示害怕。有綠拇指的人，會對於栽培植物很在行。還有，白色的謊言並不是一件很糟糕的事。」

"I don't understand. Please give me an example."

「我不懂。請舉例給我聽。」

"For example, I offer you some cake, but you don't like it. You don't say that. Instead, you say, 'No, thanks. I'm not hungry.' That's a white lie."

「例如，我給妳一些蛋糕，但是妳並不喜歡。妳不會這樣說。反之，妳會說：『不了，謝謝。我不餓。』這就是善意的謊言。」

"Oh, I see. Thanks for the explanation."

「喔，我懂了。謝謝妳的說明。」

** ──────────────

reply〔rɪˈplaɪ〕*v.* 回答　everyday〔ˈɛvrɪˈde〕*adj.* 日常的
sad〔sæd〕*adj.* 傷心的　afraid〔əˈfred〕*adj.* 害怕的
grow〔gro〕*v.* 種植　plant〔plænt〕*n.* 植物
understand〔ˌʌndɚˈstænd〕*v.* 了解；懂
example〔ɪgˈzæmpl̩〕*n.* 例子　***for example*** 例如
offer〔ˈɔfɚ〕*v.* 提供；給　instead〔ɪnˈstɛd〕*adv.* 取而代之；反之
hungry〔ˈhʌŋgrɪ〕*adv.* 餓的　see〔si〕*v.* 了解
explanation〔ˌɛkspləˈneʃən〕*n.* 解釋；說明

12. *The Girl in the Store*

I was walking around aimlessly on the ground floor of Selfridges, the big store on Oxford Street, when my eyes fell upon a beautiful girl nicely dressed in a suede coat with a white fur hood.

---

around 〔əˈraʊnd〕
aimlessly 〔ˈemlɪslɪ〕
ground floor
Oxford 〔ˈɑksfɚd〕
fall upon
nicely 〔ˈnaɪslɪ〕
dress 〔drɛs〕
suede 〔swed〕
coat 〔kot〕
fur 〔fɝ〕
hood 〔hʊd〕

The girl had large, round, blue eyes and a pretty mouth. She was slender and moved gracefully. I just couldn't take my eyes off her. Suddenly, she shocked me. She picked up an expensive silver watch from the gift counter and quietly put it into her pocket....

---

pretty [ˈprɪtɪ]
slender [ˈslɛndɚ]
gracefully [ˈgresfəlɪ]
shock [ʃɑk]
expensive [ɪkˈspɛnsɪv]
gift [gɪft]
quietly [ˈkwaɪətlɪ]

mouth [maʊθ]
move [muv]
suddenly [ˈsʌdn̩lɪ]
pick up
silver [ˈsɪlvɚ]
counter [ˈkaʊntɚ]
pocket [ˈpɑkɪt]

I was confused. Then I began to wonder: Had it really happened? Could I believe my eyes? I was pretty sure, but not absolutely certain. Should I tell the boss or call the police?

---

confused〔 kən'fjuzd 〕

wonder〔'wʌndɚ 〕 happen〔'hæpən 〕

believe〔 bə'liv 〕 pretty〔'prɪtɪ 〕

absolutely〔'æbsə,lutlɪ 〕 certain〔'sɝtn̩ 〕

boss〔 bɔs 〕 police〔 pə'lis 〕

I was still confused about what to do, when suddenly a voice called out, "Cut!" Then a fat, red-faced man came up to me and shouted angrily, "What do you think you are doing? You've ruined the best shot in the whole film!"

---

voice [vɔɪs]
cut [kʌt]
come up to
angrily ['æŋgrɪlɪ]
shot [ʃɑt]
film [fɪlm]
call out
red-faced ['rɛd'fest]
shout [ʃaʊt]
ruin ['ruɪn]
whole [hol]

12. The Girl in the Store
商店裡的女孩

中文翻譯

I was walking around aimlessly on the ground floor of Selfridges, the big store on Oxford Street, when my eyes fell upon a beautiful girl nicely dressed in a suede coat with a white fur hood.

我正在塞福瑞吉的一樓，漫無目的地閒逛，這家大商店位於牛津街上，那時我的目光落在一個美麗的女孩身上，她穿得很漂亮，她穿著麂皮製的外套，戴著一頂白色的毛皮兜帽。

The girl had large, round, blue eyes and a pretty mouth. She was slender and moved gracefully. I just couldn't take my eyes off her. Suddenly, she shocked me. She picked up an expensive silver watch from the gift counter and quietly put it into her pocket....

那女孩有雙又大又圓的藍色眼睛，而且嘴巴也很漂亮。她很苗條，而且一舉一動都很優雅。我眞的無法把目光從她身上移開。突然間，她讓我大吃一驚。她從禮品專櫃，拿起一只昂貴的銀錶，並悄悄地將它放進口袋中…

** ―――――――――――――――

around〔ə'raʊnd〕*adv.* 到處　aimlessly〔'emlɪslɪ〕*adv.* 無目的地
ground floor 一樓　Oxford〔'ɑksfəd〕*n.* 牛津　eye〔aɪ〕*n.* 眼神；目光
nicely dressed 穿得很漂亮的　suede〔swed〕*adj.* 麂皮的
fur〔fɝ〕*adj.* 毛皮的　hood〔hʊd〕*n.* 兜帽
slender〔'slɛndə〕*adj.* 苗條的　move〔muv〕*v.* 移動
gracefully〔'gresfəlɪ〕*adv.* 優雅地　***take one's eyes off***… 使目光離開…
suddenly〔'sʌdn̩lɪ〕*adv.* 突然地　shock〔ʃɑk〕*v.* 使震驚　***pick up*** 拿起
silver〔'sɪlvə〕*adj.* 銀製的　counter〔'kaʊntə〕*n.* 櫃檯
quietly〔'kwaɪətlɪ〕*adv.* 悄悄地　pocket〔'pɑkɪt〕*n.* 口袋

I was confused. Then I began to wonder: Had it really happened? Could I believe my eyes? I was pretty sure, but not absolutely certain. Should I tell the boss or call the police?

我感到很困惑。然後我開始懷疑：眞的有發生這件事嗎？我能相信自己的眼睛嗎？我很確定，但不是絕對地肯定。我該告訴老闆或是叫警察嗎？

I was still confused about what to do, when suddenly a voice called out, "Cut!" Then a fat, red-faced man came up to me and shouted angrily, "What do you think you are doing? You've ruined the best shot in the whole film!"

我仍然很困惑，不知該怎麼做，突然有個聲音大叫，「卡！」然後，一個肥胖、滿臉通紅的男人走到我身邊，他憤怒地吼叫著：「你知道你幹了什麼好事嗎？你破壞了整部電影中最好的鏡頭！」

** ———————————————

confused〔kənˈfjuzd〕*adj.* 困惑的
wonder〔ˈwʌndɚ〕*v.* 感到懷疑　pretty〔ˈprɪtɪ〕*adv.* 很
absolutely〔ˈæbsəˌlutlɪ〕*adv.* 絕對地　certain〔ˈsɜtn̩〕*adj.* 肯定的
boss〔bɔs〕*n.* 老闆　***the police*** 警方　voice〔vɔɪs〕*n.* 聲音
call out 大聲呼叫　cut〔kʌt〕*v.* 停止攝影
come up to… 走到…的身邊　shout〔ʃaʊt〕*v.* 吼叫
angrily〔ˈæŋgrɪlɪ〕*adv.* 憤怒地　ruin〔ˈruɪn〕*v.* 破壞
shot〔ʃɑt〕*n.*（影片的）拍攝　whole〔hol〕*adj.* 整個的
film〔fɪlm〕*n.* 電影

13. Nature Can Help Us Learn Many Secrets

The world of nature has many secrets. In fact — there are so many secrets, and they are so fascinating that tens of thousands of men and women and boys and girls are busy studying them.

---

nature〔ˈnetʃɚ〕
world〔wɝld〕
fascinating〔ˈfæsn̩ˌetɪŋ〕
tens of thousands of
secret〔ˈsikrɪt〕
in fact
thousand〔ˈθaʊzn̩d〕

All around us are birds, animals, insects and plants. The facts about how they live and grow are extremely interesting.

Did you know that a very famous president of the United States spent hours and hours studying birds?

---

around [əˈraʊnd]
insect [ˈɪnsɛkt]
fact [fækt]
extremely [ɪkˈstrimlɪ]
famous [ˈfeməs]
hour [aʊr]
animal [ˈænəml̩]
plant [plænt]
grow [gro]
interesting [ˈɪntrɪstɪŋ]
president [ˈprɛzədənt]

Also, a businessman who lives near Los Angeles became so interested in insects that he began to collect them. He now has over one thousand various kinds carefully preserved in glass cases.

---

also 〔ˈɔlso〕

businessman 〔ˈbɪznɪsˌmən〕

Los Angeles 〔lɔs ˈændʒələs〕

interested 〔ˈɪntrɪstɪd〕

collect 〔kəˈlɛkt〕

various 〔ˈvɛrɪəs〕

kind 〔kaɪnd〕

carefully 〔ˈkɛrfəlɪ〕

preserve 〔prɪˈzɝv〕

glass 〔glæs〕

case 〔kes〕

Now, please join me with your Science Book, and I will help you discover a few of Nature's secrets. Let us go quietly through the forests and meadows. Here we shall learn how one rabbit tells the other rabbits that there is danger.

---

join 〔 dʒɔɪn 〕
science 〔ˈsaɪəns 〕
discover 〔 dɪˈskʌvɚ 〕
a few of
quietly 〔ˈkwaɪətlɪ 〕
through 〔 θru 〕
forest 〔ˈfɔrɪst 〕
meadow 〔ˈmɛdo 〕
rabbit 〔ˈræbɪt 〕
danger 〔ˈdendʒɚ 〕

We'll carefully follow a mother bear and her young ones as they search for food and prepare for their long winter sleep.

---

follow 〔ˈfɑlo〕
mother bear
search 〔sɝtʃ〕
prepare 〔prɪˈpɛr〕
sleep 〔slip〕
bear 〔bɛr〕
young 〔jʌŋ〕
food 〔fud〕
winter 〔ˈwɪntɚ〕

We'll be able to watch bees dancing

in the air to signal to the other bees

where they can find food.

---

watch〔wɑtʃ〕

bee〔bi〕

dance〔dæns〕

air〔ɛr〕

in the air

signal〔ˈsɪgnl̩〕

find〔faɪnd〕

I plan to show you many other really neat things, but the most important thing that I can teach you is how to keep your eyes and ears open when you go outdoors. Nature tells her secret only to those who look and listen mindfully.

---

plan (plæn)	show (ʃo)
neat (nit)	important (ɪmˈpɔrtn̩t)
teach (titʃ)	keep (kip)
ear (ɪr)	outdoors (ˈaʊtˈdorz)
listen (ˈlɪsn̩)	mindfully (ˈmaɪndfəlɪ)

13. Nature Can Help Us Learn Many Secrets
大自然可以使我們得知許多秘密

中文翻譯

The world of nature has many secrets. In fact—there are so many secrets, and they are so fascinating that tens of thousands of men and women and boys and girls are busy studying them. All around us are birds, animals, insects and plants. The facts about how they live and grow are extremely interesting.

自然界中有許多奧秘。事實上——自然界有許多秘密，而且那些秘密都很有趣，所以有好幾萬的男女老少都忙著研究它們。在我們的四周，有鳥、動物、昆蟲，以及植物。它們的生活與成長情形，也是非常有趣的。

Did you know that a very famous president of the United States spent hours and hours studying birds?

你知道美國有一位非常著名的總統，花了好幾個鐘頭的時間在研究鳥類嗎？

** ——————————————

nature〔ˈnetʃɚ〕*n.* 大自然；自然界　learn〔lɝn〕*v.* 學習；知道
secret〔ˈsikrɪt〕*n.* 秘密　world〔wɝld〕*n.* 界　***in fact*** 事實上
fascinating〔ˈfæsn̩ˌetɪŋ〕*adj.* 很有趣的　thousand〔ˈθaʊzn̩d〕*n.* 千
tens of thousands of 好幾萬的　study〔ˈstʌdɪ〕*v.* 研究
insect〔ˈɪnsɛkt〕*n.* 昆蟲　plant〔plænt〕*n.* 植物　fact〔fækt〕*n.* 事實
grow〔gro〕*v.* 成長　extremely〔ɪkˈstrimlɪ〕*adv.* 非常
famous〔ˈfeməs〕*adj.* 有名的　president〔ˈprɛzədənt〕*n.* 總統
the United States 美國　***hours and hours*** 好幾個鐘頭

Also, a businessman who lives near Los Angeles became so interested in insects that he began to collect them. He now has over one thousand various kinds carefully preserved in glass cases.

還有一位住在洛杉磯附近的商人，對昆蟲很感興趣，所以他開始收集昆蟲。如今，他已經擁有一千多種不同品種的昆蟲，他把牠們小心地保存在玻璃盒中。

Now, please join me with your Science Book, and I will help you discover a few of Nature's secrets. Let us go quietly through the forests and meadows. Here we shall learn how one rabbit tells the other rabbits that there is danger.

現在，帶著你的自然科學課本跟我來，我將幫助你發現一些大自然的奧秘。讓我們悄悄地穿過森林和草地。在這裡，我們將知道兔子如何把危險的訊息告訴其他兔子。

** ———————————

also〔ˈɔlso〕*adv.* 還有　businessman〔ˈbɪznɪsˌmən〕*n.* 商人
Los Angeles〔lɔs ˈændʒələs〕*n.* 洛杉磯　become〔bɪˈkʌm〕*v.* 變得
interested〔ˈɪntrɪstɪd〕*adj.* 感興趣的　***so…that~*** 如此…以致於~
collect〔kəˈlɛkt〕*v.* 收集　various〔ˈvɛrɪəs〕*adj.* 不同的
kind〔kaɪnd〕*n.* 種類　preserve〔prɪˈzɜv〕*v.* 保存
case〔kes〕*n.* 盒子；容器　join〔dʒɔɪn〕*v.* 加入
science〔ˈsaɪəns〕*adj.* 自然科學的　discover〔dɪˈskʌvɚ〕*v.* 發現
a few of 一些　***go through*** 穿過
quietly〔ˈkwaɪətlɪ〕*adv.* 悄悄地　forest〔ˈfɔrɪst〕*n.* 森林
meadow〔ˈmɛdo〕*n.* 草地　rabbit〔ˈræbɪt〕*n.* 兔子
danger〔ˈdendʒɚ〕*n.* 危險

We'll carefully follow a mother bear and her young ones as they search for food and prepare for their long winter sleep. We'll be able to watch bees dancing in the air to signal to the other bees where they can find food. I plan to show you many other really neat things, but the most important thing that I can teach you is how to keep your eyes and ears open when you go outdoors. Nature tells her secret only to those who look and listen mindfully.

我們將小心地跟著母熊和小熊，看牠們如何覓食，以及爲漫長的冬眠作準備。我們會看到蜜蜂一邊在空中飛舞，一邊發出信號，告訴其他蜜蜂可以去哪裡覓食。我打算告訴你們其他許多很棒的事物，但在我能夠教導你們的事情當中，最重要的就是，當你到戶外時，要張大眼睛和耳朵。唯有注意觀察和聆聽的人，才能聽見大自然傾訴她的秘密。

** ——————————

follow〔ˈfɑlo〕*v.* 跟隨　***mother bear*** 母熊
young〔jʌŋ〕*adj.* 年幼的　***search for*** 尋找
food〔fud〕*n.* 食物　prepare〔prɪˈpɛr〕*v.* 準備
winter sleep 冬眠　bee〔bi〕*n.* 蜜蜂　dance〔dæns〕*v.* 跳舞
in the air 在空中　signal〔ˈsɪgnḷ〕*v.* 發出信號
plan〔plæn〕*v.* 打算　show〔ʃo〕*v.* 使明白；告知
neat〔nit〕*adj.* 很棒的　important〔ɪmˈpɔrtṇt〕*adj.* 重要的
teach〔titʃ〕*v.* 教導　keep〔kip〕*v.* 使維持（某種狀態）
ear〔ɪr〕*n.* 耳朵　outdoors〔ˈaʊtˈdorz〕*adv.* 在戶外
listen〔ˈlɪsṇ〕*v.* 聽　mindfully〔ˈmaɪndfəlɪ〕*adv.* 注意地

14. Unlucky Man

It was a dark moonless night. A man was riding alone on a bicycle without lights.

---

unlucky〔ʌn'lʌkɪ〕	dark〔dɑrk〕
moonless〔'munlɪs〕	ride〔raɪd〕
alone〔ə'lon〕	bicycle〔'baɪsɪkḷ〕
without〔wɪð'aʊt〕	light〔laɪt〕

He came up to an intersection and did not know which direction to turn. He got down from his bike and looked around for help.

---

come up to

intersection〔ˌɪntɚˈsɛkʃən〕

direction〔dəˈrɛkʃən〕

turn〔tɝn〕

bike〔baɪk〕

get down

look around

Then he saw a tall pole with a white paper on the top. It looked like a sign or something. He looked in his bag for

a lighter or matches. He found a box of matches. Luckily, one match was left.

---

pole (pol)
sign (saɪn)
bag (bæg)
match (mætʃ)
leave (liv)

top (tɑp)
or something
lighter (ˈlaɪtɚ)
luckily (ˈlʌkɪlɪ)

He climbed all the way up to the top of the pole. There he lit the precious match and read the words in the dim light. They said, "Wet Paint."

---

climb〔klaɪm〕	***all the way***
light〔laɪt〕	precious〔ˈprɛʃəs〕
read〔rid〕	word〔wɝd〕
dim〔dɪm〕	say〔se〕
wet〔wɛt〕	paint〔pent〕
wet paint	

14. Unlucky Man
倒楣的人

中文翻譯

It was a dark moonless night. A man was riding alone on a bicycle without lights. He came up to an intersection and did not know which direction to turn. He got down from his bike and looked around for help.

那是個沒有月亮的黑夜。一名男子正獨自騎著一輛沒有車燈的腳踏車。他來到了一個十字路口，卻不知該往哪個方向轉。他從腳踏車上下來，四處張望求援。

Then he saw a tall pole with a white paper on the top. It looked like a sign or something.

然後，他看見一根柱子，柱子的頂端有張白紙。那張紙看起來像是告示之類的東西。

** ——————————————

unlucky (ʌnˈlʌkɪ) *adj.* 不幸的；倒楣的　dark (dɑrk) *adj.* 黑暗的
moonless (ˈmunlɪs) *adj.* 沒有月亮的　ride (raɪd) *v.* 騎；乘
alone (əˈlon) *adv.* 獨自　bicycle (ˈbaɪsɪkḷ) *n.* 腳踏車
without (wɪðˈaʊt) *prep.* 沒有　***come up to*** 來到
intersection (ˌɪntəˈsɛkʃən) *n.* 十字路口
direction (dəˈrɛkʃən) *n.* 方向　turn (tɝn) *v.* 轉向
get down 下來　bike (baɪk) *n.* 腳踏車　***look around*** 四處張望
pole (pol) *n.* 柱子　top (tɑp) *n.* 頂端　***look like*** 看起來像
sign (saɪn) *n.* 告示；標誌　***or something*** 或什麼的

He looked in his bag for a lighter or matches. He found a box of matches. Luckily, one match was left.

他往袋子裡看，尋找打火機或火柴。他找到了一盒火柴。很幸運地，裡面還剩一根火柴棒。

He climbed all the way up to the top of the pole. There he lit the precious match and read the words in the dim light. They said, "Wet Paint."

他一直往上爬到柱子的頂端。他在那裡點燃了那根珍貴的火柴，並在昏暗的光線中讀那些字，上面寫著：「油漆未乾。」

**

look in 往…裡面看一下　bag〔bæg〕*n.* 袋子
lighter〔ˈlaɪtɚ〕*n.* 打火機　match〔mætʃ〕*n.* 火柴
luckily〔ˈlʌkɪlɪ〕*adv.* 幸運地　leave〔liv〕*v.* 遺留
climb〔klaɪm〕*v.* 爬　***all the way*** 一直；一路
light〔laɪt〕*v.* 點燃【過去式及過去分詞皆爲 lit〔lɪt〕】 *n.* 光線
precious〔ˈprɛʃəs〕*adj.* 珍貴的　read〔rid〕*v.* 讀
word〔wɝd〕*n.* 字　dim〔dɪm〕*adj.* 昏暗的
say〔se〕*v.* 寫著
wet〔wɛt〕*adj.* 未乾的
paint〔pent〕*n.* 油漆
wet paint 油漆未乾

15. Maybe Your Friend Is in That Carpet

A man goes into a store, and a clerk comes to him and says, "Are you looking for something?"

The man does not say anything for a moment, but then he quickly says, "Yes——I want a——carpet."

---

maybe [ˈmebɪ]	carpet [ˈkɑrpɪt]
clerk [klɝk]	***look for***
moment [ˈmomənt]	***for a moment***
then [ðɛn]	quickly [ˈkwɪklɪ]

The salesperson takes him to the carpets and unrolls a pretty one. The man looks at it and says, "No, thank you, I don't like that one."

The clerk unrolls another attractive carpet, but the man says, "No, thank you." again.

---

salesperson〔ˈselz,pɝsn̩〕

unroll〔ʌnˈrol〕　　pretty〔ˈprɪtɪ〕

attractive〔əˈtræktɪv〕　　again〔əˈgɛn〕

The clerk unrolls all the carpets except one, and then the man says, "Actually I don't need a carpet. I'm waiting for my best friend. She's going to meet me in your store at twelve o'clock."

---

except 〔ɪk'sɛpt〕　actually 〔'æktʃuəlɪ〕
need 〔nid〕　wait 〔wet〕
best 〔bɛst〕　meet 〔mit〕

The clerk was not angry at all! She said, "There is one more carpet here. Maybe your friend is in it. I'm going to unroll it and look in it, too."

---

not…at all angry〔'æŋgrɪ〕

15. Maybe Your Friend Is in That Carpet
也許你的朋友在那塊地毯裡

中文翻譯

A man goes into a store, and a clerk comes to him and says, "Are you looking for something?"

一位男士走進一家店，店員上前問他說：「你要找什麼嗎？」

The man does not say anything for a moment, but then he quickly says, "Yes—I want a—carpet."

那個人沉默了一會兒，然後很快地說：「是的──我想買──地毯。」

The salesperson takes him to the carpets and unrolls a pretty one. The man looks at it and says, "No, thank you, I don't like that one."

店員帶他到放地毯的地方，並攤開一張漂亮的地毯。那個人看了一下說：「不，謝謝，我不喜歡那張。」

** ───────────────

maybe〔ˈmebɪ〕*adv.* 也許　carpet〔ˈkɑrpɪt〕*n.* 地毯
clerk〔klɝk〕*n.* 店員　moment〔ˈmomənt〕*n.* 片刻；一會兒
for a moment 一會兒　quickly〔ˈkwɪklɪ〕*adv.* 很快地
salesperson〔ˈselzˌpɝsn̩〕*n.* 店員
unroll〔ʌnˈrol〕*v.* 攤開　pretty〔ˈprɪtɪ〕*adj.* 漂亮的

The clerk unrolls another attractive carpet, but the man says, "No, thank you." again.

店員又攤開另一張漂亮的地毯，但是那個人又說「不，謝謝你。」

The clerk unrolls all the carpets except one, and then the man says, "Actually I don't need a carpet. I'm waiting for my best friend. She's going to meet me in your store at twelve o'clock."

那位店員攤開了所有的地毯，只剩下一張沒攤開，然後那個人才說：「事實上，我並不需要地毯。我在等我的好朋友。她將在十二點時，到你們這家店和我碰面。」

The clerk was not angry at all! She said, "There is one more carpet here. Maybe your friend is in it. I'm going to unroll it and look in it, too."

店員一點都沒有生氣！她說：「這裡還剩下一張地毯，也許你的朋友會在裡面。我把它也攤開來瞧瞧。」

**

attractive〔əˈtræktɪv〕*adj.* 吸引人的；漂亮的
except〔ɪkˈsɛpt〕*prep.* 除了…之外　then〔ðɛn〕*adv.* 然後
actually〔ˈæktʃuəlɪ〕*adv.* 事實上　need〔nid〕*v.* 需要
wait〔wet〕*v.* 等待
best〔bɛst〕*adj.* 最好的
meet〔mit〕*v.* 和…見面
angry〔ˈæŋgrɪ〕*adj.* 生氣的
not…at all 一點也不…

16. Fishing

I enjoy fishing very much. Every weekend I get up at dawn and go to a river by bicycle about three miles from my home. I have to walk part of the way because you cannot ride through the forest areas.

---

fishing ('fɪʃɪŋ)
weekend ('wik'ɛnd)
dawn (dɔn)
bicycle ('baɪsɪkḷ)
through (θru)
area ('ɛrɪə)

fish (fɪʃ)
get up
river ('rɪvɚ)
mile (maɪl)
forest ('fɔrɪst)

Recently my wife decided that she wanted to join me and asked me to take her with me. As there were two of us, we went by car as far as we could go and then walked through the woods to the river.

---

recently [ˈrisn̩tlɪ]
wife [waɪf]
decide [dɪˈsaɪd]
join [dʒɔɪn]
as far as
woods [wʊdz]

Upon arriving, we both sat down and I started to fish. After two hours of trying, I had caught nothing.

"Why don't you teach me how and let me have a try?" my wife said.

"OK," I replied.

---

upon (ə'pɑn)

arrive (ə'raɪv)

try (traɪ)

catch (kætʃ)

teach (titʃ)

let (lɛt)

have a try

reply (rɪ'plaɪ)

She started fishing and caught six big fat fish within half an hour!

"I'll take them home first and cook them for lunch. You can take the bus home later," she said.

---

fat [fæt]
half [hæf]
cook [kʊk]
later ['letɚ]
within [wɪð'ɪn]
hour [aʊr]
lunch [lʌntʃ]

I remained at the river but caught only an old shoe. It was embarrassing. I arrived home and felt a little uncomfortable. I thought that I was the fisherman in the family!

---

remain〔rɪˈmen〕 shoe〔ʃu〕

embarrassing〔ɪmˈbærəsɪŋ〕

uncomfortable〔ʌnˈkʌmfɚtəbḷ〕

fisherman〔ˈfɪʃɚmən〕

But the fish tasted delicious. When the next Sunday arrived, I asked my wife if she wanted to go fishing again.

---

taste 〔 test 〕
delicious 〔 dɪˈlɪʃəs 〕
next 〔 nɛkst 〕
Sunday 〔ˈsʌnde 〕
again 〔 əˈgɛn 〕

"Oh, no!" she said cleverly. "You'd better let me stay at home. I'm not interested in fishing at all."

---

cleverly 〔ˈklɛvɚlɪ〕	***had better V.***
let 〔lɛt〕	stay 〔ste〕
interested 〔ˈɪntrɪstɪd〕	***not…at all***

16. Fishing
釣 魚

中文翻譯

I enjoy fishing very much. Every weekend I get up at dawn and go to a river by bicycle about three miles from my home. I have to walk part of the way because you cannot ride through the forest areas.

我很喜歡釣魚。每個週末，我都一大早就起床，然後騎著腳踏車到離家大約三哩外的河邊釣魚。我必須步行一段路，因爲無法騎著腳踏車穿過森林。

Recently my wife decided that she wanted to join me and asked me to take her with me. As there were two of us, we went by car as far as we could go and then walked through the woods to the river.

最近我太太決定跟我一起去釣魚，所以她要求我帶她一塊兒去。因爲有兩個人，所以我們就開車到車子可以到達的地方，然後走路穿過森林到河邊。

** ─────────────────────

fishing〔ˈfɪʃɪŋ〕*n.* 釣魚　fish〔fɪʃ〕*v.* 釣魚　*n.* 魚
weekend〔ˈwikˈɛnd〕*n.* 週末　***get up*** 起床　dawn〔dɔn〕*n.* 黎明
river〔ˈrɪvɚ〕*n.* 河流　bicycle〔ˈbaɪsɪkl̩〕*n.* 腳踏車
mile〔maɪl〕*n.* 哩　ride〔raɪd〕*v.* 騎；搭乘
through〔θru〕*prep.* 穿越　forest〔ˈfɔrɪst〕*n.* 森林
area〔ˈɛrɪə〕*n.* 區域　recently〔ˈrisn̩tlɪ〕*adv.* 最近
wife〔waɪf〕*n.* 太太　decide〔dɪˈsaɪd〕*v.* 決定
join〔dʒɔɪn〕*v.* 加入；和（某人）一起做同樣的事
as〔əz〕*conj.* 因爲　***as far as*** 遠到　woods〔wʊdz〕*n.pl.* 森林

Upon arriving, we both sat down and I started to fish. After two hours of trying, I had caught nothing.	一抵達河邊，我們倆都坐下，接著我開始釣魚。試了兩個小時以後，我什麼也沒釣到。
"Why don't you teach me how and let me have a try?" my wife said.	「你爲什麼不敎我怎麼釣，讓我也試試？」我的太太說。
"OK," I replied.	「好吧，」我回答說。
She started fishing and caught six big fat fish within half an hour!	她開始釣魚，並且在半小時內就釣到六條大肥魚！
"I'll take them home first and cook them for lunch. You can take the bus home later," she said.	「我先把牠們帶回家，然後把牠們煮來當午餐。你可以晚點再搭公車回家，」她說。

＊＊ ——————————

upon〔əˈpɑn〕*prep.* 一…（就～）　arrive〔əˈraɪv〕*v.* 抵達
try〔traɪ〕*v. n.* 嘗試　catch〔kætʃ〕*v.* 抓到
teach〔titʃ〕*v.* 敎導　how〔haʊ〕*n.* 方法
have a try 試試看　reply〔rɪˈplaɪ〕*v.* 回答
within〔wɪðˈɪn〕*prep.* 在…之內　half〔hæf〕*adj.* 一半的
hour〔aʊr〕*n.* 小時　take〔tek〕*v.* 拿；搭乘
cook〔kʊk〕*v.* 烹調；煮　lunch〔lʌntʃ〕*n.* 午餐
later〔ˈletɚ〕*adv.* 較晚地

I remained at the river but caught only an old shoe. It was embarrassing. I arrived home and felt a little uncomfortable. I thought that I was the fisherman in the family! But the fish tasted delicious. When the next Sunday arrived, I asked my wife if she wanted to go fishing again.

我繼續留在河邊，但卻只釣到一隻舊鞋。眞糗。我回到家之後，覺得有點不自在。我還以爲自己是家中唯一會釣魚的人呢！但是，這些魚嚐起來非常美味。當下個星期天來臨時，我問我太太要不要再跟我一塊去釣魚。

"Oh, no!" she said cleverly. "You'd better let me stay at home. I'm not interested in fishing at all."

「哦，不！」她聰明地回答說。「你最好讓我留在家裡。我對釣魚一點興趣也沒有。」

**

remain〔rɪ'men〕*v.* 停留；留在
shoe〔ʃu〕*n.* 鞋子
embarrassing〔ɪm'bærəsɪŋ〕*adj.* 令人尷尬的
uncomfortable〔ʌn'kʌmfɚtəbl̩〕*adj.* 不自在的
fisherman〔'fɪʃɚmən〕*n.* 漁夫；釣魚的人
taste〔test〕*v.* 嚐起來　delicious〔dɪ'lɪʃəs〕*adj.* 美味的
Sunday〔'sʌnde〕*n.* 星期天　cleverly〔'klɛvɚlɪ〕*adv.* 聰明地
had better V. 最好～　stay〔ste〕*v.* 停留
interested〔'ɪntrɪstɪd〕*adj.* 感興趣的　***not…at all*** 一點也不…

17. He Also Needed It

A forgetful minister was traveling on a train.

The conductor came by and asked him to show his ticket.

---

also〔ˈɔlso〕
forgetful〔fɚˈgɛtfəl〕
travel〔ˈtrævḷ〕
conductor〔kənˈdʌktɚ〕
show〔ʃo〕
need〔nid〕
minister〔ˈmɪnɪstɚ〕
train〔tren〕
come by
ticket〔ˈtɪkɪt〕

The minister searched in his pockets and bags but could not find it.

"Oh, don't worry about it now, sir," said the conductor. "You'll come across it later."

---

search (sɝtʃ)

pocket ('pɑkɪt)

bag (bæg)

worry ('wɝɪ)

come across

later ('letɚ)

"But—" said the minister, continuing his search.

"Really, that's all right," said the other. "I can wait. I don't mind."

---

continue (kən'tɪnjʊ)

That's all right.

mind (maɪnd)

really ('riəlɪ)

wait (wet)

"But I do," said the minister. "I have to find the ticket immediately."

"Why is that?" said the conductor.

"Because," answered the minister, "I don't know where I am going. I have completely forgot my destination."

---

immediately〔ɪ'midɪɪtlɪ〕
completely〔kəm'plitlɪ〕
destination〔,dɛstə'neʃən〕
answer〔'ænsɚ〕
forget〔fɚ'gɛt〕

17. He Also Needed It

他也需要它

中文翻譯

A forgetful minister was traveling on a train.

一位健忘的牧師搭火車旅行。

The conductor came by and asked him to show his ticket.

查票員經過他身邊，並要求他出示車票。

The minister searched in his pockets and bags but could not find it.

牧師搜遍了口袋和手提袋，但都找不到車票。

"Oh, don't worry about it now, sir," said the conductor. "You'll come across it later."

「喔，先生，現在不用擔心車票，」查票員說。「你待會就會找到了。」

** ——————————————

also〔ˈɔlso〕*adv.* 也
need〔nid〕*v.* 需要　forgetful〔fɚˈgɛtfəl〕*adj.* 健忘的
minister〔ˈmɪnɪstɚ〕*n.* 牧師　travel〔ˈtrævḷ〕*v.* 旅行
train〔tren〕*n.* 火車　conductor〔kənˈdʌktɚ〕*n.* 車掌；查票員
come by 經過　show〔ʃo〕*v.* 出示　ticket〔ˈtɪkɪt〕*n.* 車票
search〔sɝtʃ〕*v.* 尋找　pocket〔ˈpɑkɪt〕*n.* 口袋
bag〔bæg〕*n.* 袋子；手提袋　worry〔ˈwɝɪ〕*v.* 擔心
come across 偶然發現　later〔ˈletɚ〕*adv.* 稍後；較晚地

"But—" said the minister, continuing his search.

「但是——」牧師一邊說一邊繼續找。

"Really, that's all right," said the other. "I can wait. I don't mind."

「眞的沒關係，」查票員說。「我可以等。我不介意。」

"But I do," said the minister. "I have to find the ticket immediately."

「但是我介意，」牧師說。「我必須立刻把車票找出來。」

"Why is that?" said the conductor.

「爲什麼呢？」查票員說。

"Because," answered the minister, "I don't know where I am going. I have completely forgot my destination."

「因爲，」牧師回答說，「我不知道我要去哪裡。我完全忘了目的地是哪裡。」

** ————————————————

continue (kən'tɪnju) *v.* 繼續　search (sɜtʃ) *n.* 搜尋
That's all right. 沒關係。　wait (wet) *v.* 等
mind (maɪnd) *v.* 介意　immediately (ɪ'midɪɪtlɪ) *adv.* 立刻
answer ('ænsɚ) *v.* 回答　completely (kəm'plitlɪ) *adv.* 完全地
forget (fɚ'gɛt) *v.* 忘記　destination (ˌdɛstə'neʃən) *n.* 目的地

18. *How We Get Day and Night*

The sun rises in the east and sets in the west. When the sun comes up, it is morning. When the sun goes down, it is evening. When the sun shines, it's daytime.

---

sun〔 sʌn 〕
east〔 ist 〕
west〔 wɛst 〕
go down
daytime〔ˈde,taɪm〕
rise〔 raɪz 〕
set〔 sɛt 〕
come up
shine〔 ʃaɪn 〕

Morning is the period of time between sunrise and twelve o'clock noon or between sunrise and lunch. At twelve o'clock, the sun is high up in the sky, over our heads. The sun is overhead at noon. We call this time "high noon."

---

period〔ˈpɪrɪəd〕
noon〔nun〕
high up
over〔ˈovɚ〕
overhead〔ˈovɚˈhɛd〕
sunrise〔ˈsʌnˌraɪz〕
lunch〔lʌntʃ〕
sky〔skaɪ〕
head〔hɛd〕
high noon

The sun shines during the day. The moon and the stars shine at night. When the sun rises, it is light outside.

It is light during the day. During the night, if the moon doesn't shine, it's dark.

---

during ('djurɪŋ) moon (mun)
star (stɑr) light (laɪt)
outside ('aut'saɪd) dark (dɑrk)

What are the days and nights like during the summer? During the summer, the days are long and the nights are short.

What about in winter? During winter the days are short and the nights are long.

---

like〔laɪk〕

What about…?

summer〔ˈsʌmɚ〕

winter〔ˈwɪntɚ〕

18. How We Get Day and Night
日夜的由來

中文翻譯

The sun rises in the east and sets in the west. When the sun comes up, it is morning. When the sun goes down, it is evening. When the sun shines, it's daytime. Morning is the period of time between sunrise and twelve o'clock noon or between sunrise and lunch. At twelve o'clock, the sun is high up in the sky, over our heads. The sun is overhead at noon. We call this time "high noon."

太陽從東方升起，從西方落下。當太陽升起時，就是早晨。太陽落下時，就是晚上。白天時陽光普照。早晨是指從日出到中午十二點的這段時間，或是從日出到午餐的這段時間。十二點時，太陽正高掛在天空，也就是我們的頭頂上方。中午的太陽就在我們頭上。我們稱這段時間爲「正午」。

** ―――――――――――――――――

sun〔sʌn〕*n.* 太陽　rise〔raɪz〕*v.* 升起　east〔ist〕*n.* 東方
set〔sɛt〕*v.* 落下　west〔wɛst〕*n.* 西方　***come up*** 上升
go down 落下　shine〔ʃaɪn〕*v.* 發光；照耀
daytime〔ˈde,taɪm〕*n.* 白天　period〔ˈpɪrɪəd〕*n.* 期間
sunrise〔ˈsʌn,raɪz〕*n.* 日出　noon〔nun〕*n.* 中午
lunch〔lʌntʃ〕*n.* 午餐　***high up*** 高高在上的　sky〔skaɪ〕*n.* 天空
over〔ˈovɚ〕*prep.* 在…上面　head〔hɛd〕*n.* 頭
overhead〔ˈovɚˈhɛd〕*adv.* 在頭上；在空中　***high noon*** 正午

The sun shines during the day. The moon and the stars shine at night. When the sun rises, it is light outside. It is light during the day. During the night, if the moon doesn't shine, it's dark.

白天時陽光普照。夜晚則是星月閃耀。當太陽升起時，外面會很明亮。白天時都很明亮。到了夜晚，如果月亮沒有散發出光輝，就會一片黑暗。

What are the days and nights like during the summer? During the summer, the days are long and the nights are short. What about in winter? During winter the days are short and the nights are long.

夏季時，日夜又是什麼樣的情形呢？夏季晝長夜短。那麼冬天呢？冬天是晝短夜長。

** ──────────────

during〔ˈdjʊrɪŋ〕*prep.* 在…期間　moon〔mun〕*n.* 月亮
star〔stɑr〕*n.* 星星　light〔laɪt〕*adj.* 明亮的
outside〔ˈaʊtˈsaɪd〕*adv.* 在外面　dark〔dɑrk〕*adj.* 黑暗的
like〔laɪk〕*prep.* 像　summer〔ˈsʌmɚ〕*n.* 夏天
What about…? …怎麼樣？　winter〔ˈwɪntɚ〕*n.* 冬天

19. Friendship Is a Treasure

We often say that we want many friends. And this is a good thing. It is good for us to have many friends. Happiness is doubled when we share it with a friend.

---

friendship〔'frɛnd,ʃɪp〕 treasure〔'trɛʒɚ〕
happiness〔'hæpɪnɪs〕 double〔'dʌbḷ〕
share〔ʃɛr〕

An old saying goes that a friend in need is a friend indeed. This means that there are two kinds of friends.

---

saying [ˈseɪŋ]
in need
mean [min]
need [nid]
indeed [ɪnˈdid]
kind [kaɪnd]

One kind of friend flees when we are in trouble. The other kind remains nearby even when there is trouble.

---

flee (fli)

be in trouble

remain (rɪ'men)

even ('ivən)

trouble ('trʌbl̩)

other ('ʌðɚ)

nearby ('nɪr'baɪ)

When I was in the sixth grade, I knew a very shy and quiet girl. She seldom spoke. She never played with anyone. She had no friends. I felt very sorry for her.

---

grade 〔 gred 〕 know 〔 no 〕
shy 〔 ʃaɪ 〕 quiet 〔ˈkwaɪət 〕
seldom 〔ˈsɛldəm 〕 sorry 〔ˈsɔrɪ 〕

Every day I tried to give her a compliment or invite her to do something. "I like

your book bag." "The color of your shirt is pretty." "Let's go to the zoo next Sunday, OK?"

---

compliment〔ˈkɑmpləmənt〕
invite〔ɪnˈvaɪt〕
color〔ˈkʌlɚ〕
shirt〔ʃɝt〕
pretty〔ˈprɪtɪ〕
zoo〔zu〕
next〔nɛkst〕
Sunday〔ˈsʌnde〕

She never said a single word to me. But on the very last day of school, she met me at the gate. She put her mouth to my ear and whispered, "Thank you for everything!"— She gave me a beautiful smile. We have been close pals ever since.

---

single [ˈsɪŋgl̩]	very [ˈvɛrɪ]
last [læst]	meet [mit]
gate [get]	mouth [maʊθ]
ear [ɪr]	whisper [ˈhwɪspɚ]
beautiful [ˈbjutəfəl]	smile [smaɪl]
close [klos]	pal [pæl]
ever since	

19. Friendship Is a Treasure
友誼是很珍貴的

中文翻譯

We often say that we want many friends. And this is a good thing. It is good for us to have many friends. Happiness is doubled when we share it with a friend.

我們常說自己想要有很多朋友。這是件好事。擁有許多朋友對我們有益。當我們跟朋友分享，快樂就會加倍。

An old saying goes that a friend in need is a friend indeed. This means that there are two kinds of friends. One kind of friend flees when we are in trouble. The other kind remains nearby even when there is trouble.

有句古老的諺語說：「患難見眞情。」這句話的意思是朋友有兩種。有一種朋友會在我們陷入困境時逃之夭夭。另一種則是在我們有困難時，仍然留在我們身邊。

** ———————————

friendship ('frɛndʃɪp) *n.* 友誼　treasure ('trɛʒɚ) *n.* 寶藏；珍貴品
happiness ('hæpɪnɪs) *n.* 快樂　double ('dʌbl̩) *v.* 加倍
share (ʃɛr) *v.* 分享　saying ('seɪŋ) *n.* 諺語
go (go) *v.* (文句等) 表達爲；寫著　need (nid) *n.* 窮困；危急之際
in need 在患難中　indeed (ɪn'did) *adv.* 眞正地
mean (min) *v.* 意思是　kind (kaɪnd) *n.* 種類
flee (fli) *v.* 逃走；避開　trouble ('trʌbl̩) *n.* 困難；麻煩
be in trouble 有麻煩；有困難　remain (rɪ'men) *v.* 停留
nearby ('nɪr'baɪ) *adv.* 在附近　even ('ivən) *adv.* 即使

When I was in the sixth grade, I knew a very shy and quiet girl. She seldom spoke. She never played with anyone. She had no friends. I felt very sorry for her. Every day I tried to give her a compliment or invite her to do something. "I like your book bag." "The color of your shirt is pretty." "Let's go to the zoo next Sunday, OK?"

我六年級時，認識了一位非常害羞文靜的女孩。她很少講話。她從不和任何人玩耍。她沒有朋友。我真為她感到難過。我每天都試著稱讚她，或是邀請她去做某件事。「我喜歡妳的書包。」「妳襯衫的顏色真漂亮。」「我們下星期天去動物園好嗎？」

She never said a single word to me. But on the very last day of school, she met me at the gate. She put her mouth to my ear and whispered, "Thank you for everything!"—She gave me a beautiful smile. We have been close pals ever since.

她從來都沒有跟我說過一句話。但就在最後一天上學時，她在校門口和我見面。她把嘴巴湊到我的耳邊低聲說：「謝謝你所做的一切！」——她笑得很美。從此，我們便成為親密的朋友。

** ──────────

grade〔gred〕*n.* 年級　know〔no〕*v.* 認識　shy〔ʃaɪ〕*adj.* 害羞的
quiet〔ˈkwaɪət〕*adj.* 文靜的　seldom〔ˈsɛldəm〕*adv.* 很少
compliment〔ˈkɑmpləmənt〕*n.* 稱讚　invite〔ɪnˈvaɪt〕*v.* 邀請
shirt〔ʃɝt〕*n.* 襯衫　pretty〔ˈprɪtɪ〕*adj.* 漂亮的　zoo〔zu〕*n.* 動物園
single〔ˈsɪŋgl̩〕*adj.* 單一的　very〔ˈvɛrɪ〕*adv.* 就是；正在
last〔læst〕*adj.* 最後的　meet〔mit〕*v.* 和…見面
gate〔get〕*n.* 大門　mouth〔maʊθ〕*n.* 嘴巴　ear〔ɪr〕*n.* 耳朵
whisper〔ˈhwɪspɚ〕*v.* 低聲說　beautiful〔ˈbjutəfəl〕*adj.* 美麗的
smile〔smaɪl〕*n.* 微笑　close〔klos〕*adj.* 親密的　pal〔pæl〕*n.* 朋友
ever since 自從…之後一直

20. Two Hours Too Early!

A wealthy man had some late-night work to do.

He called his servant and said to him, “I’ll be up late tonight. Please wake me at 6 a.m. tomorrow morning.”

---

hour〔 aʊr 〕
wealthy〔ˈwɛlθɪ 〕
servant〔ˈsɝvənt 〕
late〔 let 〕
wake〔 wek 〕
tomorrow〔 təˈmɔro 〕
early〔ˈɝlɪ 〕
late-night〔ˈletˌnaɪt 〕
up〔 ʌp 〕
tonight〔 təˈnaɪt 〕
a.m.〔ˈeˈɛm 〕

He felt like he had only slept a little while when his servant aroused him.

"Six o'clock already?" asked the gentleman, rubbing his sleepy eyes.

---

feel like	sleep〔slip〕
while〔hwaɪl〕	arouse〔əˈraʊz〕
already〔ɔlˈrɛdɪ〕	gentleman〔ˈdʒɛntl̩mən〕
rub〔rʌb〕	sleepy〔ˈslipɪ〕

"No, it is only four a.m., sir," answered the servant.

"I thought I told you to wake me at six," said the master. "Why did you wake me so early?"

sir [sɝ]

answer ['ænsɚ]

master ['mæstɚ]

"Well," said the servant. "I only came to tell you that you still have two hours to sleep."

---

well ﹝wɛl﹞ tell ﹝tɛl﹞
still ﹝stɪl﹞

20. Two Hours Too Early!
早兩個小時！

中文翻譯

A wealthy man had some late-night work to do.

有個有錢人要熬夜工作。

He called his servant and said to him, “I'll be up late tonight. Please wake me at 6 a.m. tomorrow morning.”

他把僕人叫來對他說：「我今晚會很晚睡。請在明天早上六點鐘叫我起床。」

He felt like he had only slept a little while when his servant aroused him.

當僕人來叫醒他時，他覺得自己才睡了一會兒。

** ———

hour〔 aʊr 〕*n.* 小時　　early〔ˈɝlɪ〕*adv.* 早
wealthy〔ˈwɛlθɪ〕*adj.* 有錢的　　late-night〔ˈletˌnaɪt〕*adj.* 深夜的
servant〔ˈsɝvənt〕*n.* 僕人　　up〔 ʌp 〕*adj.* 沒睡覺的
late〔 let 〕*adv.* 晚　　tonight〔 təˈnaɪt 〕*adv.* 今晚
wake〔 wek 〕*v.* 叫醒　　a.m.〔ˈeˈɛm 〕*adv.* 早上
tomorrow〔 təˈmɔro 〕*n.* 明天
feel like 覺得像　　sleep〔 slip 〕*v.* 睡覺
while〔 hwaɪl 〕*n.*（短暫的）時間　　arouse〔 əˈraʊz 〕*v.* 喚醒

"Six o'clock already?" asked the gentleman, rubbing his sleepy eyes.

「已經六點了嗎？」那位先生邊揉著還很想睡的眼睛邊問。

"No, it is only four a.m., sir," answered the servant.

「不，先生，現在才早上四點，」僕人回答。

"I thought I told you to wake me at six," said the master. "Why did you wake me so early?"

「我以為我跟你說六點再叫我，」主人說。「你為什麼這麼早叫醒我？」

"Well," said the servant. "I only came to tell you that you still have two hours to sleep."

「嗯，」僕人說。「我只是來告訴你，你還有兩個鐘頭可以睡。」

** ——————————————

already〔ɔlˈrɛdɪ〕*adv.* 已經
gentleman〔ˈdʒɛntḷmən〕*n.* 先生；男士
rub〔rʌb〕*v.* 摩擦；揉　　sleepy〔ˈslipɪ〕*adj.* 想睡的
sir〔sɝ〕*n.* 先生　　answer〔ˈænsɚ〕*v.* 回答
well〔wɛl〕*interj.* 嗯　　tell〔tɛl〕*v.* 告訴
still〔stɪl〕*adv.* 還；仍然

21. A Most Forgetful Couple

Mr. and Mrs. Jones are a very absent-minded couple. For example, Mr. Jones sometimes goes to his company to work on Sunday morning because he thinks it is Monday. And Mrs. Jones sometimes forgets to make meals for the family.

---

forgetful (fɚ'gɛtfəl) couple ('kʌpl̩)
absent-minded ('æbsn̩t'maɪndɪd)
sometimes ('sʌm,taɪmz) company ('kʌmpənɪ)
forget (fɚ'gɛt) meal (mil)

One winter holiday they made a plan to travel to London by plane. The Jones arrived at the airport only ten minutes before the plane was due to depart!

---

winter [ˈwɪntɚ]	plan [plæn]
travel [ˈtrævl̩]	London [ˈlʌndən]
plane [plen]	arrive [əˈraɪv]
airport [ˈɛrˌport]	minute [ˈmɪnɪt]
due [dju]	depart [dɪˈpɑrt]

But suddenly Mrs. Jones said that she had to tell their daughter Sally to remember to lock the front door when she leaves for school every day. As Sally was at school then, they couldn't reach her on the phone.

---

suddenly〔ˈsʌdn̩lɪ〕

daughter〔ˈdɔtɚ〕

remember〔rɪˈmɛmbɚ〕

lock〔lɑk〕

front〔frʌnt〕

leave for

then〔ðɛn〕

reach〔ritʃ〕

phone〔fon〕

So they hurried to the post office. Mrs. Jones quickly wrote a short note to Sally. Mr. Jones bought a stamp and an envelope and dropped the letter into the mailbox.

---

hurry〔ˈhɝɪ〕
office〔ˈɔfɪs〕
quickly〔ˈkwɪklɪ〕
note〔not〕
envelope〔ˈɛnvə,lop〕
letter〔ˈlɛtɚ〕
post〔post〕
post office
write〔raɪt〕
stamp〔stæmp〕
drop〔drɑp〕
mailbox〔ˈmel,bɑks〕

When they returned to the airport, they had only two minutes before the plane was going to leave. Suddenly, Mrs. Jones started crying. Why?

---

return〔 rɪˈtɝn 〕 start〔 stɑrt 〕

cry〔 kraɪ 〕

The short note to her daughter was still in her hands. She had put their plane tickets into the envelope and then dropped it into the mailbox.

---

still〔 stɪl 〕　　hand〔 hænd 〕

ticket〔ˈtɪkɪt 〕

21. A Most Forgetful Couple
非常健忘的夫婦

中文翻譯

Mr. and Mrs. Jones are a very absent-minded couple. For example, Mr. Jones sometimes goes to his company to work on Sunday morning because he thinks it is Monday. And Mrs. Jones sometimes forgets to make meals for the family.

瓊斯夫婦是一對非常健忘的夫妻。舉例來說，瓊斯先生有時會在星期天早上去公司上班，因爲他以爲那天是星期一。而瓊斯太太有時候則會忘了煮飯給家人吃。

One winter holiday they made a plan to travel to London by plane. The Jones arrived at the airport only ten minutes before the plane was due to depart!

在一個冬季的假日，他們計畫搭飛機到倫敦旅行。瓊斯夫妻在班機預定起飛前十分鐘，才抵達機場！

** ——————————————

most〔most〕*adv.* 非常（= *very*）　forgetful〔fɚˈgɛtfəl〕*adj.* 健忘的
couple〔ˈkʌpl̩〕*n.* 夫婦　absent-minded〔ˈæbsn̩tˈmaɪndɪd〕*adj.* 健忘的
for example 舉例來說　sometimes〔ˈsʌm,taɪmz〕*adv.* 有時候
company〔ˈkʌmpənɪ〕*n.* 公司　forget〔fɚˈgɛt〕*v.* 忘記
meal〔mil〕*n.* 一餐　winter〔ˈwɪntɚ〕*adj.* 冬天的
plan〔plæn〕*n.* 計畫　travel〔ˈtrævl̩〕*v.* 旅行
London〔ˈlʌndən〕*n.* 倫敦　plane〔plen〕*n.* 飛機
arrive〔əˈraɪv〕*v.* 抵達　airport〔ˈɛr,port〕*n.* 機場
minute〔ˈmɪnɪt〕*n.* 分鐘　***be to V.*** 即將要…
due〔dju〕*adj.* 預定的　depart〔dɪˈpɑrt〕*v.* 出發；離開

But suddenly Mrs. Jones said that she had to tell their daughter Sally to remember to lock the front door when she leaves for school every day. As Sally was at school then, they couldn't reach her on the phone. So they hurried to the post office. Mrs. Jones quickly wrote a short note to Sally. Mr. Jones bought a stamp and an envelope and dropped the letter into the mailbox. When they returned to the airport, they had only two minutes before the plane was going to leave. Suddenly, Mrs. Jones started crying. Why? The short note to her daughter was still in her hands. She had put their plane tickets into the envelope and then dropped it into the mailbox.

但是瓊斯太太突然說，她必須告訴她們的女兒莎莉，要記得每天出門上學時，把前門鎖好。因爲當時莎莉正在上學，他們沒辦法用電話連絡到她。所以，他們急忙趕到郵局。瓊斯太太很快地寫了封短信給莎莉。瓊斯先生則買了郵票及信封，然後把信投入郵筒。當他們回到機場時，離飛機起飛只剩下兩分鐘了。突然間，瓊斯太太哭了起來。爲什麼呢？因爲給女兒的短信還在她手裡。她把他們的飛機票放進信封裡，並且把它丟進郵筒了。

** ——————————————

suddenly〔ˈsʌdn̩lɪ〕*adv.* 突然地　daughter〔ˈdɔtɚ〕*n.* 女兒
remember〔rɪˈmɛmbɚ〕*v.* 記得　lock〔lɑk〕*v.* 鎖上
front〔frʌnt〕*adj.* 前面的　***leave for*** 動身前往　as〔əs〕*conj.* 因爲
then〔ðɛn〕*adv.* 那時　reach〔ritʃ〕*v.* 連絡　phone〔fon〕*n.* 電話
hurry〔ˈhɝɪ〕*v.* 趕往　***post office*** 郵局　quickly〔ˈkwɪklɪ〕*adv.* 很快地
note〔not〕*n.* 短箋；短信　stamp〔stæmp〕*n.* 郵票
envelope〔ˈɛnvə͵lop〕*n.* 信封　drop〔drɑp〕*v.* 把…投入
letter〔ˈlɛtɚ〕*n.* 信　mailbox〔ˈmel͵bɑks〕*n.* 郵筒
return〔rɪˈtɝn〕*v.* 回到　ticket〔ˈtɪkɪt〕*n.* 票

22. The Snake Translator

A Chinese gentleman returning from Java brought a number of Javanese snakes with him. He kept them in a glass case and told his assistant to take care of them.

---

snake ﹝snek﹞
Chinese ﹝tʃaɪ'niz﹞
return ﹝rɪ'tɝn﹞
a number of
keep ﹝kip﹞
case ﹝kes﹞
take care of
translator ﹝træns'letɚ﹞
gentleman ﹝'dʒɛntḷmən﹞
Java ﹝'dʒɑvə﹞
Javanese ﹝ˌdʒævə'niz﹞
glass ﹝glæs﹞
assistant ﹝ə'sɪstənt﹞

One day

one of the snakes got away and could not be found. "My boss will be furious with me when he returns," said the assistant to himself.

---

one day

find ﹝faɪnd﹞

furious ﹝ˈfjʊrɪəs﹞

get away

boss ﹝bɔs﹞

say to *oneself*

So he put an ordinary grass snake in the case in place of the missing one.

When the gentleman returned, he went to the case and saw the common snake.

---

ordinary [ˈɔrdn̩ˌɛrɪ]

grass snake

in place of

missing [ˈmɪsɪŋ]

common [ˈkɑmən]

"How did this snake get in here?" he said. "It is just a common grass snake."

"That is so, sir," replied the assistant. "I put it there as a translator, because all the others are foreigners."

---

get in　　　　reply〔rɪ'plaɪ〕

foreigner〔'fɔrɪnɚ〕

22. The Snake Translator
蛇翻譯員

中文翻譯

A Chinese gentleman returning from Java brought a number of Javanese snakes with him. He kept them in a glass case and told his assistant to take care of them.

有個中國人從爪哇帶回了一些爪哇蛇。他把牠們養在玻璃盒裡，並叫他的助手照顧牠們。

One day one of the snakes got away and could not be found. "My boss will be furious with me when he returns," said the assistant to himself.

有一天，有一條蛇跑了，而且找不到。「老闆回來的時候一定會很生氣，」這位助手自言自語說。

** ————————————————

snake〔snek〕*n.* 蛇　translator〔træns'letɚ〕*n.* 翻譯員
Chinese〔tʃaɪ'niz〕*adj.* 中國的
gentleman〔'dʒɛntḷmən〕*n.* 先生；男士　return〔rɪ'tɝn〕*v.* 回來
Java〔'dʒɑvə〕*n.* 爪哇　***a number of*** 一些；許多
Javanese〔,dʒævə'niz〕*adj.* 爪哇的　keep〔kip〕*v.* 飼養
glass〔glæs〕*adj.* 玻璃的　case〔kes〕*n.* 盒子
assistant〔ə'sɪstənt〕*n.* 助手　***take care of*** 照顧　***one day*** 有一天
get away 逃脫　find〔faɪnd〕*v.* 找到　boss〔bɔs〕*n.* 老闆
furious〔'fjʊrɪəs〕*adj.* 狂怒的　***say to** oneself* 自言自語

So he put an ordinary grass snake in the case in place of the missing one.

所以他把一條普通的草蛇放進盒子裡，來取代那條失蹤的蛇。

When the gentleman returned, he went to the case and saw the common snake.

當那位先生回來時，他走近盒子，然後看見了那條普通的蛇。

"How did this snake get in here?" he said. "It is just a common grass snake."

「這條蛇怎麼會跑進來這裡？」他說。「這只是條普通的草蛇。」

"That is so, sir," replied the assistant. "I put it there as a translator, because all the others are foreigners."

「確實是這樣，先生，」助手回答。「我把牠放在那裡當翻譯員，因爲其他蛇都是外國蛇。」

** ______________________________

ordinary〔ˈɔrdn̩ˌɛrɪ〕*adj.* 普通的
grass snake 草蛇（一種無毒小蛇）
in place of 取代
missing〔ˈmɪsɪŋ〕*adj.* 失蹤的
common〔ˈkɑmən〕*adj.* 普通的　　***get in*** 進入
reply〔rɪˈplaɪ〕*v.* 回答　　foreigner〔ˈfɔrɪnɚ〕*n.* 外國人

23. Heads or Tails, You Lose

It was twelve at night, and I was returning home. The footsteps that followed behind me through the dark back streets of New York City were those of two young guys who appeared to be up to no good.

---

heads 〔 hɛdz 〕
lose 〔 luz 〕
footstep 〔ˈfʊt,stɛp 〕
behind 〔 bɪˈhaɪnd 〕
dark 〔 dɑrk 〕
guy 〔 gaɪ 〕
be up to no good

tails 〔 telz 〕
return 〔 rɪˈtɝn 〕
follow 〔ˈfɑlo 〕
through 〔 θru 〕
back street
appear 〔 əˈpɪr 〕

I walked faster, but the steps behind me became faster, too. I tried to stop a cab that passed by, but the driver either didn't see me or was afraid to stop. The steps came closer and closer. I'm not a man who gets scared easily, but I must say I was a bit worried now.

---

step 〔 stɛp 〕

become 〔 bɪ'kʌm 〕

stop 〔 stɑp 〕

cab 〔 kæb 〕

pass by

afraid 〔 ə'fred 〕

scared 〔 skɛrd 〕

easily 〔'izɪlɪ 〕

bit 〔 bɪt 〕

worried 〔'wɝɪd 〕

At last the two young men caught up with me. “Pardon me, sir, could you please lend us a penny?” said one of them in a clear voice which sounded nice enough and made me feel a lot less nervous.

---

at last
pardon 〔ˈpɑrdn̩〕
penny 〔ˈpɛnɪ〕
voice 〔vɔɪs〕
a lot
nervous 〔ˈnɝvəs〕

catch up with
lend 〔lɛnd〕
clear 〔klɪr〕
sound 〔saʊnd〕
less 〔lɛs〕

"Sure, no problem," I said. And to let them know that I was not afraid I added, "But can I ask you why you need it?"

"Of course, sir," answered the other. "We'd like to flip the coin to see which of us will steal your watch, and which your wallet."

---

sure〔ʃur〕
add〔æd〕
answer〔ˈænsɚ〕
coin〔kɔɪn〕
wallet〔ˈwɑlɪt〕
problem〔ˈprɑbləm〕
need〔nid〕
flip〔flɪp〕
steal〔stil〕

23. Heads or Tails, You Lose
不論正面或反面，你都是輸

中文翻譯

It was twelve at night, and I was returning home. The footsteps that followed behind me through the dark back streets of New York City were those of two young guys who appeared to be up to no good.

當時是晚上十二點，我正在回家的路上。跟在我後面穿過紐約市偏僻暗巷的腳步聲，是來自兩個看起來就不懷好意的年輕小夥子。

I walked faster, but the steps behind me became faster, too. I tried to stop a cab that passed by, but the driver either didn't see me or was afraid to stop. The steps came closer and closer.

我加快腳步，但是身後的步伐也跟著加快。我試著攔下一輛經過我身邊的計程車，但司機不是沒看到我，就是因爲害怕而不敢停車。腳步聲越來越近。

** ——————————————

heads〔hɛdz〕*n.*（擲硬幣時）硬幣的正面　tails〔telz〕*n.* 硬幣的反面
lose〔luz〕*v.* 輸　return〔rɪˈtɝn〕*v.* 返回
footstep〔ˈfʊtˌstɛp〕*n.* 腳步聲　behind〔bɪˈhaɪnd〕*prep.* 在…後面
dark〔dɑrk〕*adj.* 黑暗的　***back street*** 偏僻的街道；後街
New York City 紐約市　guy〔gaɪ〕*n.*（男）人
appear〔əˈpɪr〕*v.* 顯得；好像是　***be up to no good*** 圖謀不軌
step〔stɛp〕*n.* 腳步；步伐　become〔bɪˈkʌm〕*v.* 變得
stop〔stɑp〕*v.* 攔下　cab〔kæb〕*n.* 計程車　***pass by*** 經過
either A ***or*** B 不是 A，就是 B

I'm not a man who gets scared easily, but I must say I was a bit worried now.

我不是個容易害怕的人，但是我必須說，我現在開始有點擔心了。

At last the two young men caught up with me. "Pardon me, sir, could you please lend us a penny?" said one of them in a clear voice which sounded nice enough and made me feel a lot less nervous. "Sure, no problem," I said. And to let them know that I was not afraid I added, "But can I ask you why you need it?" "Of course, sir," answered the other. "We'd like to flip the coin to see which of us will steal your watch, and which your wallet."

最後那兩個年輕人追上了我。「對不起，先生，可以請你借給我們一分錢嗎？」其中一個人用聽起來又清楚，又有善意的聲音說，而這讓我覺得不那麼緊張了。「好的，沒問題，」我說。爲了讓他們知道我並不害怕，我接著說：「但是我可以問一下，你們要它做什麼嗎？」「當然，先生。」另外一個人回答。「我們想要用丟銅板來決定，誰偷你的錶，還有誰偷你的皮夾。」

** ——————————————

scared〔skɛrd〕*adj.* 害怕的　***a bit*** 有點　worried〔ˈwɝɪd〕*adj.* 擔心的
at last 最後　***catch up with*** 趕上　***Pardon me.*** 對不起。
sir〔sɝ〕*n.* 先生　lend〔lɛnd〕*v.* 借（出）
penny〔ˈpɛnɪ〕*n.* 一分硬幣　clear〔klɪr〕*adj.* 清楚的
voice〔vɔɪs〕*n.* 聲音　sound〔saund〕*v.* 聽起來
less〔lɛs〕*adv.* 較不　nervous〔ˈnɝvəs〕*adj.* 緊張的
sure〔ʃur〕*adv.* 好　***No problem.*** 沒問題。
add〔æd〕*v.* 補充地說；又說　need〔nid〕*v.* 需要
answer〔ˈænsɚ〕*v.* 回答　flip〔flɪp〕*v.* 將（硬幣）拋上去
coin〔kɔɪn〕*n.* 硬幣　steal〔stil〕*v.* 偷　wallet〔ˈwalɪt〕*n.* 皮夾

24. The Face That Launched a Thousand Ships

Homer is a poet who is world famous. All over the world we can find people who enjoy his stories.

---

face 〔 fes 〕

thousand 〔ˈθaʊznd̩ 〕

Homer 〔ˈhomɚ 〕

famous 〔ˈfeməs 〕

enjoy 〔 ɪnˈdʒɔɪ 〕

launch 〔 lɔntʃ 〕

ship 〔 ʃɪp 〕

poet 〔ˈpo·ɪt 〕

all over the world

Homer wrote stories about the enchantingly beautiful Queen Helen.

She was the world's most beautiful woman.

---

enchantingly〔ɪn'tʃæntɪŋlɪ〕
beautiful〔'bjutəfəl〕 queen〔kwin〕
woman〔'wumən〕

She was abducted from her home in Sparta. She was taken to the famous city of Troy. The king of Sparta got together many men and ships. They went to Troy to get Helen back.

---

abduct 〔 æb′dʌkt 〕 Sparta 〔′spɑrtə 〕
Troy 〔 trɔɪ 〕 king 〔 kɪŋ 〕
get together

The men of Troy were very strong. The soldiers who came to fight from Sparta fought for a decade, without success. So they decided to try a trick.

---

strong〔 strɔŋ 〕	soldier〔'soldʒɚ〕
fight〔 faɪt 〕	decade〔'dɛked 〕
without〔 wɪð'aʊt 〕	success〔 sək'sɛs 〕
decide〔 dɪ'saɪd 〕	trick〔 trɪk 〕

They made a huge wooden horse.

On it they wrote, "A gift to your gods."

Then they left. The people of Troy admired the horse. They took the horse into the city.

---

huge (hjudʒ) wooden (ˈwudn̩)
horse (hɔrs) gift (gɪft)
god (gɑd) then (ðɛn)
leave (liv) admire (ədˈmaɪr)

But they didn't know that inside the horse the best soldiers were hiding. Late that night they opened the gates to the city. The whole Spartan army attacked. They destroyed the whole city. Helen went back to her king.

---

inside〔ˈɪnˈsaɪd〕
hide〔haɪd〕
late〔let〕
gate〔get〕
whole〔hol〕
Spartan〔ˈspɑrtn̩〕
army〔ˈɑrmɪ〕
attack〔əˈtæk〕
destroy〔dɪˈstrɔɪ〕

24. The Face That Launched a Thousand Ships
一張發動千軍萬馬的臉

中文翻譯

Homer is a poet who is world famous. All over the world we can find people who enjoy his stories.

荷馬是位名滿天下的詩人。我們可以在世界各地找到喜愛他的故事的人。

Homer wrote stories about the enchantingly beautiful Queen Helen. She was the world's most beautiful woman. She was abducted from her home in Sparta. She was taken to the famous city of Troy. The king of Sparta got together many men and ships. They went to Troy to get Helen back.

荷馬寫了一些故事，是關於那位迷人的美麗皇后海倫。她是這個世界上最美的女人。她從斯巴達的家鄉被拐走。她被帶到了著名的城市特洛伊。斯巴達的國王召集了許多人還有船。他們前往特洛伊去把海倫帶回來。

** ———

face〔fes〕*n.* 臉　launch〔lɔntʃ〕*v.* 發動；展開
thousand〔ˈθaʊzn̩d〕*n.* 一千　ship〔ʃɪp〕*n.* 船
Homer〔ˈhomɚ〕*n.* 荷馬【古希臘詩人】　poet〔ˈpo·ɪt〕*n.* 詩人
famous〔ˈfeməs〕*adj.* 有名的　***all over the world*** 在全世界
enjoy〔ɪnˈdʒɔɪ〕*v.* 喜歡　enchantingly〔ɪnˈtʃæntɪŋlɪ〕*adv.* 迷人地
beautiful〔ˈbjutəfəl〕*adj.* 美麗的　queen〔kwin〕*n.* 皇后
abduct〔æbˈdʌkt〕*v.* 拐走　Sparta〔ˈspɑrtə〕*n.* 斯巴達【古希臘城邦】
Troy〔trɔɪ〕*n.* 特洛伊【小亞細亞西北部古城】　***get together*** 聚集；集合

The men of Troy were very strong. The soldiers who came to fight from Sparta fought for a decade, without success. So they decided to try a trick.

特洛伊人非常強壯。從斯巴達前來作戰的士兵，打了十年的仗，仍然無法戰勝。因此他們決定試試看用詭計。

They made a huge wooden horse. On it they wrote, "A gift to your gods." Then they left. The people of Troy admired the horse. They took the horse into the city. But they didn't know that inside the horse the best soldiers were hiding. Late that night they opened the gates to the city. The whole Spartan army attacked. They destroyed the whole city. Helen went back to her king.

他們造了一隻巨大的木馬。在上面寫著「獻給你們的神的禮物」。接著他們就離開了。特洛伊人非常喜歡這隻木馬。他們把木馬拖進城裡。但是他們並不知道，木馬裡藏著最勇猛的士兵。當晚深夜，那些士兵打開了城門。斯巴達全軍發動攻擊。他們摧毀了整座城市。海倫又回到了她的國王身邊。

** ──────────

strong〔strɔŋ〕*adj.* 強壯的　soldier〔'soldʒɚ〕*n.* 士兵
fight〔faɪt〕*v.* 作戰　decade〔'dɛked〕*n.* 十年
without〔wɪð'aʊt〕*prep.* 沒有　success〔sək'sɛs〕*n.* 成功
decide〔dɪ'saɪd〕*v.* 決定　trick〔trɪk〕*n.* 詭計；計謀
huge〔hjudʒ〕*adj.* 巨大的　wooden〔'wʊdn̩〕*adj.* 木製的
horse〔hɔrs〕*n.* 馬　gift〔gɪft〕*n.* 禮物　god〔gɑd〕*n.* 神
then〔ðɛn〕*adv.* 然後　leave〔liv〕*v.* 離開
admire〔əd'maɪr〕*v.* 讚賞；喜歡　inside〔'ɪn'saɪd〕*prep.* 在…裡面
hide〔haɪd〕*v.* 躲藏　late〔let〕*adv.* 晚　gate〔get〕*n.* 大門
whole〔hol〕*adj.* 全部的　Spartan〔'spɑrtn̩〕*adj.* 斯巴達的
army〔'ɑrmɪ〕*n.* 軍隊　attack〔ə'tæk〕*v.* 攻擊
destroy〔dɪ'strɔɪ〕*v.* 摧毀

25. The Amazing Earthworm

The earthworm is a helpful animal. Above the ground, it is food for other animals.

Underground, it makes the soil rich for fields and gardens.

---

amazing〔 ə'mezɪŋ 〕 earthworm〔'ɝθ,wɝm 〕
helpful〔'hɛlpfəl 〕 animal〔'ænəml̩ 〕
above〔 ə'bʌv 〕 ground〔 graʊnd 〕
food〔 fud 〕
underground〔'ʌndɚ'graʊnd 〕
soil〔 sɔɪl 〕 rich〔 rɪtʃ 〕
field〔 fild 〕 garden〔'gɑrdn̩ 〕

Earthworms dig small holes that loosen the soil and make it easy for air and water to reach the roots of the plants. These holes help keep the soil well drained.

---

dig 〔dɪg〕
loosen 〔ˈlusn̩〕
root 〔rut〕
keep 〔kip〕
hole 〔hol〕
reach 〔ritʃ〕
plant 〔plænt〕
drain 〔dren〕

Earthworms take dead leaves, sticks, and even grass into their tunnels.

When this plant material decays, it makes the soil very fertile.

---

dead (dɛd)
leaves (livz)
stick (stɪk)
even ('ivən)
grass (græs)
tunnel ('tʌnl̩)
material (mə'tɪrɪəl)
decay (dɪ'ke)
fertile ('fɝtl̩)

The earthworm is the most useful animal in building up good topsoil. It is calculated that in one year over fifty thousand earthworms carry almost twenty tons of high quality soil to the surface of an acre of land. Amazingly, one worm possibly adds three fourths of a pound of dirt to the topsoil.

---

topsoil (ˈtɑp,sɔɪl)　calculate (ˈkælkjə,let)

quality (ˈkwɑlətɪ)　surface (ˈsɝfɪs)

acre (ˈekɚ)　amazingly (əˈmezɪŋlɪ)

possibly (ˈpɑsəblɪ)　pound (paʊnd)

dirt (dɝt)

25. The Amazing Earthworm
不可思議的蚯蚓

中文翻譯

The earthworm is a helpful animal. Above the ground, it is food for other animals. Underground, it makes the soil rich for fields and gardens.

蚯蚓是有益的動物。在地面上，牠是其他動物的食物。在地底下，牠爲田地和花園製造出肥沃的土壤。

Earthworms dig small holes that loosen the soil and make it easy for air and water to reach the roots of the plants. These holes help keep the soil well drained.

蚯蚓所鑽出的許多小洞，使土壤變鬆，所以空氣和水可以輕易地到達植物根部。這些洞有助於讓土壤保持排水良好。

** ───────────────

amazing〔əˈmezɪŋ〕*adj.* 驚人的；不可思議的
earthworm〔ˈɝθˌwɝm〕*n.* 蚯蚓 helpful〔ˈhɛlpfəl〕*adj.* 有益的
animal〔ˈænəml̩〕*n.* 動物 above〔əˈbʌv〕*prep.* 在…之上
ground〔graʊnd〕*n.* 地面 food〔fud〕*n.* 食物
underground〔ˈʌndɚˈgraʊnd〕*adv.* 在地下 soil〔sɔɪl〕*n.* 土壤
rich〔rɪtʃ〕*adj.* 肥沃的 field〔fild〕*n.* 田地
garden〔ˈgɑrdn̩〕*n.* 花園 dig〔dɪg〕*v.* 挖掘 hole〔hol〕*n.* 洞
loosen〔ˈlusn̩〕*v.* 翻鬆 reach〔ritʃ〕*v.* 到達 root〔rut〕*n.* 根部
plant〔plænt〕*n.* 植物 keep〔kip〕*v.* 保持 drain〔dren〕*v.* 排水
well drained 排水設備良好的

Earthworms take dead leaves, sticks, and even grass into their tunnels. When this plant material decays, it makes the soil very fertile.

蚯蚓把枯葉、枯枝，還有甚至是青草，都搬進牠們的地道中。當這些植物腐敗後，會使土壤變得非常肥沃。

The earthworm is the most useful animal in building up good topsoil. It is calculated that in one year over fifty thousand earthworms carry almost twenty tons of high quality soil to the surface of an acre of land. Amazingly, one worm possibly adds three fourths of a pound of dirt to the topsoil.

蚯蚓是建立優良表土層最有用的動物。根據估計，在一英畝的土地上，一年會有五萬多隻蚯蚓，把將近二十噸的沃土帶到表層上。令人驚訝的是，一隻蚯蚓可能就爲表土層增加了四分之三磅的土壤。

** ——————————

dead〔dɛd〕*adj.* 枯萎的　leaves〔livz〕*n. pl.* 樹葉【單數爲 leaf〔lif〕】
stick〔stɪk〕*n.* 枯枝　even〔'ivən〕*adv.* 甚至　grass〔græs〕*n.* 草
tunnel〔'tʌnḷ〕*n.* 地道　material〔mə'tɪrɪəl〕*n.* 材料；物質
decay〔dɪ'ke〕*v.* 腐爛　fertile〔'fɝtḷ〕*adj.* 肥沃的
useful〔'jusfəl〕*adj.* 有用的；有益的　***build up*** 建立；形成
topsoil〔'tɑp,sɔɪl〕*n.* 表土層　calculate〔'kælkjə,let〕*v.* 計算；估計
over〔'ovɚ〕*prep.* 超過　thousand〔'θaʊzṇd〕*adj.* 一千的
carry〔'kærɪ〕*v.* 搬運　almost〔'ɔl,most〕*adv.* 幾乎　ton〔tʌn〕*n.* 噸
quality〔'kwɑlətɪ〕*n.* 品質　surface〔'sɝfɪs〕*n.* 表面
acre〔'ekɚ〕*n.* 英畝　land〔lænd〕*n.* 土地
amazingly〔ə'mezɪŋlɪ〕*adv.* 令人驚訝的是　worm〔wɝm〕*n.* 蟲
possibly〔'pɑsəblɪ〕*adv.* 可能　add〔æd〕*v.* 增加
three fourths 四分之三　pound〔paund〕*n.* 磅　dirt〔dɝt〕*n.* 土壤

26. The Next Speaker Listens Well

There was a presentation with two guest speakers and a large crowd. In the beginning, the first speaker was fascinating,

---

next〔 nɛkst 〕 speaker〔ˈspikɚ 〕
listen〔ˈlɪsn̩ 〕 presentation〔ˌprɛzn̩ˈteʃən 〕
guest〔 gɛst 〕 large〔 lɑrdʒ 〕
crowd〔 kraʊd 〕 beginning〔 bɪˈgɪnɪŋ 〕
fascinating〔ˈfæsn̩ˌetɪŋ 〕

but soon after, he became rather boring. First one person got up from his chair and left the room. Then another disappeared, and so forth. The speaker didn't pay attention to this; he just went on with his speech.

---

soon (sun)
rather ('ræðɚ)
boring ('bɔrɪŋ)
get up
leave (liv)
disappear (ˌdɪsə'pɪr)
and so forth
attention (ə'tɛnʃən)
pay attention to
go on with
speech (spitʃ)

Finally, when he was through, there was only one person sitting in the auditorium.

The speaker got down from the stage and talked to the man:

---

finally (ˈfaɪnḷɪ)
through (θru)
auditorium (ˌɔdəˈtorɪəm)
get down
stage (stedʒ)

"Thank you so much for remaining here when all the others left the room."

"Oh, think nothing of it," replied the man. "I can not leave like everybody else, because I am the next speaker."

---

remain (rɪ'men)
reply (rɪ'plaɪ)
Think nothing of it.
else (ɛls)

26. The Next Speaker Listens Well
下一位演講者最專心聽

中文翻譯

There was a presentation with two guest speakers and a large crowd. In the beginning, the first speaker was fascinating, but soon after, he became rather boring. First one person got up from his chair and left the room. Then another disappeared, and so forth. The speaker didn't pay attention to this; he just went on with his speech.

有一場演講邀請了兩位演講者，及一群聽衆。剛開始時，第一位演講者非常風趣，但不久之後，他就變得非常無趣。第一個人從椅子上站了起來，然後離開了房間。接著，其他人也紛紛離開。演講者並沒有注意到這件事情；他只是繼續他的演講。

** ——————————

next (nɛkst) *adj.* 下一個的　speaker (ˈspikɚ) *n.* 演講者
listen (ˈlɪsn̩) *v.* 聽　presentation (ˌprɛzn̩ˈteʃən) *n.* 發表會
guest (gɛst) *adj.* 被邀請的　large (lɑrdʒ) *adj.* 衆多的
crowd (kraʊd) *n.* 群衆　beginning (bɪˈgɪnɪŋ) *n.* 開始
in the beginning 一開始　fascinating (ˈfæsn̩ˌetɪŋ) *adj.* 迷人的；很有趣的
soon after 不久之後　rather (ˈræðɚ) *adv.* 非常
boring (ˈbɔrɪŋ) *adj.* 無聊的　***get up*** 站起來　leave (liv) *v.* 離開
disappear (ˌdɪsəˈpɪr) *v.* 消失　***and so forth*** 等等　***pay attention to*** 注意
go on with 繼續　speech (spitʃ) *n.* 演講

Finally, when he was through, there was only one person sitting in the auditorium.

最後，當他結束時，聽衆席上只剩下一個人坐著。

The speaker got down from the stage and talked to the man: "Thank you so much for remaining here when all the others left the room."

那名演講者從台上走了下來，並對那個人說：「非常感謝你還留在這裡，尤其是當其他人都離開這個房間時。」

"Oh, think nothing of it," replied the man. "I can not leave like everybody else, because I am the next speaker."

「喔，不用客氣，」那個人回答說。「我不能像其他人一樣離開，因爲我是下一個演講者。」

** ———

finally〔ˈfaɪnḷɪ〕*adv.* 最後
through〔θru〕*adv.* 完成；結束
auditorium〔ˌɔdəˈtorɪəm〕*n.* 聽衆席
get down 下來　　stage〔stedʒ〕*n.* 講台
remain〔rɪˈmen〕*v.* 停留
Think nothing of it. 別放在心上；不客氣。
reply〔rɪˈplaɪ〕*v.* 回答　　else〔ɛls〕*adj.* 其他的

27. The Indians Were First

Indians were the first true Native Americans. They lived in peace with everything in nature.

Indian ('ɪndɪən)	true (tru)
native ('netɪv)	American (ə'mɛrɪkən)
peace (pis)	nature ('netʃɚ)

Then Europeans come across the ocean. They cut down many trees and killed many animals. They made villages, farms, roads, and cities.

The Indians, who still followed traditional ways, soon lost their land.

European 〔ˌjurəˈpiən〕	***come across***
ocean 〔ˈoʃən〕	***cut down***
kill 〔kɪl〕	village 〔ˈvɪlɪdʒ〕
farm 〔fɑrm〕	follow 〔ˈfɑlo〕
traditional 〔trəˈdɪʃənl̩〕	soon 〔sun〕
lose 〔luz〕	land 〔lænd〕

Nowadays most American Indians live like other Americans. Many Indians have forgotten their past customs.

nowadays 〔'naʊə,dez〕

past 〔pæst〕

forget 〔fɚ'gɛt〕

custom 〔'kʌstəm〕

But there are some Indians who still respect the old ways. They speak their old languages, tell their old tales, and dance their old dances. Indians are an important part of America. They have been there from the beginning. They still have much to teach us about living in harmony with nature.

---

still (stɪl)
respect (rɪ'spɛkt)
language ('læŋgwɪdʒ)
tale (tel)
dance (dæns)
important (ɪm'pɔrtn̩t)
America (ə'mɛrɪkə)
from the beginning
teach (titʃ)
harmony ('hɑrmənɪ)

27. The Indians Were First

印地安人最早來

中文翻譯

Indians were the first true Native Americans. They lived in peace with everything in nature. Then Europeans come across the ocean. They cut down many trees and killed many animals. They made villages, farms, roads, and cities. The Indians, who still followed traditional ways, soon lost their land.

印地安人是最早的，而且是眞正的美國原住民。他們和自然界萬物和平共存。接著歐洲人跨海而來。他們砍伐許多樹木，並殺死很多動物。他們建造了村莊、農場、道路，以及城市。而仍舊依循傳統生活方式的印地安人，很快便失去了他們的土地。

** ________________________________

Indian〔ˈɪndɪən〕*n.* 美國印地安人　true〔tru〕*adj.* 眞正的
native〔ˈnetɪv〕*adj.* 生於本地的
American〔əˈmɛrɪkən〕*n.* 美國人　*adj.* 美國的
Native American 印地安人　peace〔pis〕*n.* 平靜；和平
nature〔ˈnetʃɚ〕*n.* 自然　European〔ˌjurəˈpiən〕*n.* 歐洲人
come across 越過　ocean〔ˈoʃən〕*n.* 海洋　***cut down*** 砍伐
kill〔kɪl〕*v.* 殺死　village〔ˈvɪlɪdʒ〕*n.* 村落　farm〔fɑrm〕*n.* 農場
follow〔ˈfɑlo〕*v.* 遵循　traditional〔trəˈdɪʃənḷ〕*adj.* 傳統的
soon〔sun〕*adv.* 很快地　lose〔luz〕*v.* 失去　land〔lænd〕*n.* 土地

Nowadays most American Indians live like other Americans. Many Indians have forgotten their past customs. But there are some Indians who still respect the old ways. They speak their old languages, tell their old tales, and dance their old dances. Indians are an important part of America. They have been there from the beginning. They still have much to teach us about living in harmony with nature.

現在，大部份的美國印地安人，也過著和其他美國人一樣的生活。許多印地安人都已經忘記了過去的習俗。但是有些印地安人仍然遵奉古老的習俗。他們說古老的語言和古老的故事，而且還跳著他們古老的舞蹈。印地安人是美國很重要的一部份。他們從一開始就在那裡了。他們還可以教我們許多如何與自然和諧共存的方法。

**

nowadays (ˈnauəˌdez) *adv.* 現在
like (laɪk) *prep.* 像　forget (fəˈgɛt) *v.* 忘記
past (pæst) *adj.* 過去的　custom (ˈkʌstəm) *n.* 習俗
respect (rɪˈspɛkt) *v.* 尊奉；尊敬
ways (wez) *n. pl.* 習俗
language (ˈlæŋgwɪdʒ) *n.* 語言
tale (tel) *n.* 故事
dance (dæns) *v.* 跳舞　*n.* 舞蹈
important (ɪmˈpɔrtn̩t) *adj.* 重要的
part (pɑrt) *n.* 部份　America (əˈmɛrɪkə) *n.* 美國
beginning (bɪˈgɪnɪŋ) *n.* 開始　teach (titʃ) *v.* 教導
harmony (ˈhɑrmənɪ) *n.* 和諧　***in harmony with*** 與…和諧一致

28. Paul Bunyan– an American Legend

Paul Bunyan is an American legend. He was a giant. So people called him Giant Paul.

Paul Bunyan 〔 pɔl ˈbʌnjən 〕

American 〔 əˈmɛrɪkən 〕

legend 〔ˈlɛdʒənd 〕 giant 〔ˈdʒaɪənt 〕

When Paul was a young student, his teacher had to say, "Paul, never put up your hand." Once when he did, he knocked a huge hole in the ceiling of the school.

---

young〔jʌŋ〕
once〔wʌns〕
huge〔hjudʒ〕
ceiling〔ˈsilɪŋ〕

put up
knock〔nɑk〕
hole〔hol〕

Paul lived in the forest. He was a master woodsman. He could cut down big trees with one chop!

He was an excellent hunter, too. He could easily kill ten running deer at a time.

---

forest〔'fɔrɪst〕

woodsman〔'wʊdzmən〕

excellent〔'ɛksḷənt〕

easily〔'izɪlɪ〕

at a time

master〔'mæstɚ〕

chop〔tʃɑp〕

hunter〔'hʌntɚ〕

deer〔dɪr〕

He had the keen eye of an expert hunter. His vision was so incredible

that he could shoot birds that were flying miles high in the sky. When they finally hit the ground, they were already spoiled!

---

keen (kin)
expert ('ɛkspɝt)
vision ('vɪʒən)
incredible (ɪn'krɛdəbl̩)
shoot (ʃut)
mile (maɪl)
finally ('faɪnl̩ɪ)
ground (graʊnd)
spoil (spɔɪl)

28. Paul Bunyan – an American Legend
保羅・班揚——美國傳奇人物

中文翻譯

Paul Bunyan is an American legend. He was a giant. So people called him Giant Paul.

保羅・班揚是美國傳奇人物。他是個巨人。所以人們稱他爲巨人保羅。

When Paul was a young student, his teacher had to say, "Paul, never put up your hand." Once when he did, he knocked a huge hole in the ceiling of the school.

當保羅還是個年輕的學生時，他的老師必須告訴他說：「保羅，不准把手舉起來。」有一次他把手舉起來，結果學校的天花板被他敲了個大洞。

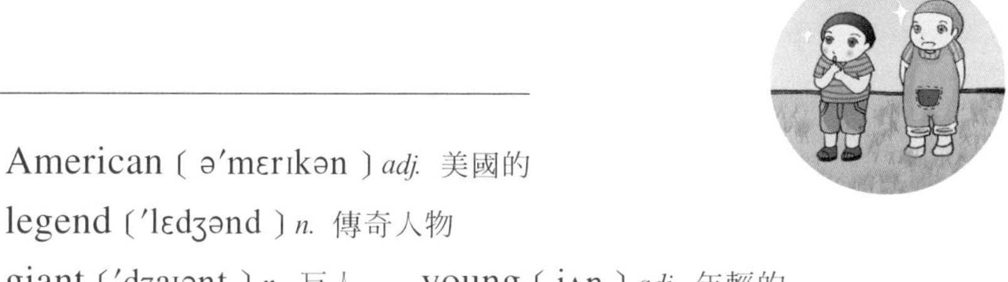

＊＊ ——————————

American〔əˈmɛrɪkən〕*adj.* 美國的
legend〔ˈlɛdʒənd〕*n.* 傳奇人物
giant〔ˈdʒaɪənt〕*n.* 巨人　　young〔jʌŋ〕*adj.* 年輕的
put up 舉起　　once〔wʌns〕*adv.* 一次
knock〔nɑk〕*v.* 敲；撞擊　　huge〔hjudʒ〕*adj.* 巨大的
hole〔hol〕*n.* 洞　　ceiling〔ˈsilɪŋ〕*n.* 天花板

Paul lived in the forest. He was a master woodsman. He could cut down big trees with one chop!

保羅住在森林裡。他是個熟練的樵夫。他能一斧將大樹砍倒！

He was an excellent hunter, too. He could easily kill ten running deer at a time.

他也是個優秀的獵人。他能輕易地一次殺死十隻奔跑中的鹿群。

He had the keen eye of an expert hunter. His vision was so incredible that he could shoot birds that were flying miles high in the sky. When they finally hit the ground, they were already spoiled!

他有著專業獵人的銳利眼神。他的視力非常好，可以射下天空中數英哩高的飛鳥。當牠們最後掉到地上時，都已經腐壞了！

** ————————————————

forest〔ˈfɔrɪst〕*n.* 森林　master〔ˈmæstɚ〕*adj.* 熟練的
woodsman〔ˈwudzmən〕*n.* 樵夫　***cut down*** 砍伐
chop〔tʃɑp〕*n.* 砍；劈　excellent〔ˈɛksḷənt〕*adj.* 優秀的
hunter〔ˈhʌntɚ〕*n.* 獵人　easily〔ˈizɪlɪ〕*adv.* 輕易地
kill〔kɪl〕*v.* 殺死　running〔ˈrʌnɪŋ〕*adj.* 在奔跑的
deer〔dɪr〕*n.* 鹿　***at a time*** 一次
keen〔kin〕*adj.* 銳利的　expert〔ˈɛkspɝt〕*adj.* 專家的
vision〔ˈvɪʒən〕*n.* 視力
incredible〔ɪnˈkrɛdəbḷ〕*adj.* 驚人的；令人無法置信的；極好的
shoot〔ʃut〕*v.* 射中　mile〔maɪl〕*n.* 英哩　sky〔skaɪ〕*n.* 天空
finally〔ˈfaɪnḷɪ〕*adv.* 最後　hit〔hɪt〕*v.* 抵達
ground〔graund〕*n.* 地面　spoil〔spɔɪl〕*v.* 使腐壞

29. No Sense of Direction

Some people are fortunate to be born with a good sense of direction. After only one visit to a place, they can find it again years later.

---

sense [sɛns]
fortunate [ˈfɔrtʃənɪt]
visit [ˈvɪzɪt]
later [ˈletɚ]
direction [dəˈrɛkʃən]
born [bɔrn]
place [ples]

I am one of the unlucky people who have an awfully poor sense of direction. I may have visited a place many times, but I still get lost and confused.

---

unlucky (ʌn'lʌkɪ)	awfully ('ɔflɪ)
poor (pʊr)	time (taɪm)
still (stɪl)	lost (lɔst)
get lost	confused (kən'fjuzd)

When I was a teen, I was too shy. I was afraid to ask strangers the way. I used to wander round in circles hoping that I might find the spot I was heading for.

---

teen〔 tin 〕	shy〔 ʃaɪ 〕
afraid〔 əˈfred 〕	stranger〔ˈstrendʒɚ 〕
used to	wander〔ˈwɑndɚ 〕
round〔 raʊnd 〕	circle〔ˈsɝkl̩ 〕
spot〔 spɑt 〕	***head for***

No longer am I too shy to ask others for directions. But I often receive such unclear replies that I feel I probably won't get to my destination.

---

no longer	receive [rɪ'siv]
such [sʌtʃ]	unclear [ʌn'klɪr]
reply [rɪ'plaɪ]	probably ['prɑbəblɪ]
get to	destination [ˌdɛstə'neʃən]

29. No Sense of Direction
沒有方向感

中文翻譯

Some people are fortunate to be born with a good sense of direction. After only one visit to a place, they can find it again years later.

有些人很幸運，一出生就有良好的方向感。只要去過一個地方一次之後，就可以在多年後，再次找到它。

I am one of the unlucky people who have an awfully poor sense of direction. I may have visited a place many times, but I still get lost and confused.

我是不幸的人之一，我的方向感非常糟糕。或許我已經到過某個地方很多次了，但是我還是會迷路，搞不清楚方向。

** ——————————————

sense〔sɛns〕*n.* 感覺　direction〔dəˈrɛkʃən〕*n.* 方向
sense of direction 方向感　fortunate〔ˈfɔrtʃənɪt〕*adj.* 幸運的
born〔bɔrn〕*adj.* 出生的　***be born with*** 生來就有
visit〔ˈvɪzɪt〕*n. v.* 拜訪；參觀　place〔ples〕*n.* 地方
later〔ˈletɚ〕*adv.* 以後　unlucky〔ʌnˈlʌkɪ〕*adj.* 不幸的
awfully〔ˈɔflɪ〕*adv.* 非常地　poor〔pur〕*adj.* 差的
time〔taɪm〕*n.* 次　lost〔lɔst〕*adj.* 迷路的
get lost 迷路　confused〔kənˈfjuzd〕*adj.* 困惑的

When I was a teen, I was too shy. I was afraid to ask strangers the way. I used to wander round in circles hoping that I might find the spot I was heading for.

當我還是個青少年時，我十分害羞。我不敢向陌生人問路。我常常一直繞著圈子，然後希望也許可以找到我要去的地方。

No longer am I too shy to ask others for directions. But I often receive such unclear replies that I feel I probably won't get to my destination.

現在我已經不會害羞到不敢向別人問路了。但是我常常得到很不清楚的回答，以致於我都覺得自己可能到不了目的地。

** ───────────────

teen〔tin〕*n.* 青少年　shy〔ʃaɪ〕*adj.* 害羞的
afraid〔ə'fred〕*adj.* 害怕的　stranger〔'strendʒɚ〕*n.* 陌生人
used to 以前常常　wander〔'wɑndɚ〕*v.* 徘徊；在…到處走
round〔raʊnd〕*adv.* 在附近；到處　circle〔'sɝkl̩〕*n.* 圓圈
hope〔hop〕*v.* 希望　spot〔spɑt〕*v.* 地點
head for 前往　***no longer*** 不再
receive〔rɪ'siv〕*v.* 得到　such〔sʌtʃ〕*adv.* 非常
unclear〔ʌn'klɪr〕*adj.* 不清楚的
reply〔rɪ'plaɪ〕*n.* 回答
probably〔'prɑbəblɪ〕*adv.* 可能　***get to*** 抵達
destination〔ˌdɛstə'neʃən〕*n.* 目的地

30. *A Lily in the Kitchen*

In ancient times the people of Egypt liked garlic very much. They would not work without garlic. They craved it every day. They also placed garlic around their necks on a string to keep away bad luck.

---

lily 〔ˈlɪlɪ〕
ancient 〔ˈenʃənt〕
Egypt 〔ˈidʒɪpt〕
garlic 〔ˈgɑrlɪk〕
crave 〔krev〕
place 〔ples〕
neck 〔nɛk〕
string 〔strɪŋ〕
luck 〔lʌk〕

Garlic is a very old plant. We can read about it in many ancient books. It was sometimes called a "lily" in the Bible, because the garlic plant is a member of the lily family. The onion plant is a similar member.

---

plant〔plænt〕
sometimes〔'sʌm,taɪmz〕　Bible〔'baɪbḷ〕
member〔'mɛmbɚ〕　family〔'fæməlɪ〕
onion〔'ʌnjən〕　similar〔'sɪməlɚ〕

Both the garlic and onion plants have a very strong odor, but garlic's smell is much stronger than onion's. Many claim that garlic's smell is the strongest smell among all foods.

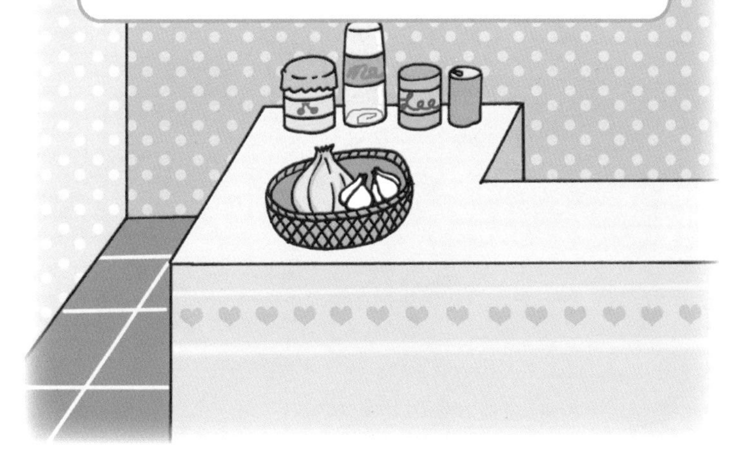

---

strong 〔 strɔŋ 〕 odor 〔ˈodɚ 〕

smell 〔 smɛl 〕 claim 〔 klem 〕

among 〔 əˈmʌŋ 〕 food 〔 fud 〕

Many folks today think that garlic is beneficial to the health. They believe that it prevents illness.

---

folks〔foks〕

beneficial〔ˌbɛnəˈfɪʃəl〕

health〔hɛlθ〕 believe〔bəˈliv〕

prevent〔prɪˈvɛnt〕 illness〔ˈɪlnɪs〕

Garlic may benefit us in one way. Its strong smell may keep away people. Because of this it may stop people from spreading

germs to each other. It is not easy at all to eliminate the smell of garlic.

---

benefit〔ˈbɛnəfɪt〕

keep away

germ〔dʒɝm〕

in one way

spread〔sprɛd〕

eliminate〔ɪˈlɪməˌnet〕

For decades people have tried to handle it. But all efforts have been in vain. Now, we know the reason why.

The smell of garlic goes into the lungs. From there it comes out. It comes out through the skin, too.

---

decade [ˈdɛked]
handle [ˈhændl̩]
effort [ˈɛfɚt]
vain [ven]
in vain
reason [ˈrizn̩]
lung [lʌŋ]
through [θru]
skin [skɪn]

30. A Lily in the Kitchen

廚房裡的百合花

中文翻譯

In ancient times the people of Egypt liked garlic very much. They would not work without garlic. They craved it every day. They also placed garlic around their necks on a string to keep away bad luck.

古代的埃及人非常喜歡大蒜。他們沒有大蒜就無法工作。他們每天都渴望吃到大蒜。他們還用線把大蒜串起來掛在脖子上，以驅除惡運。

Garlic is a very old plant. We can read about it in many ancient books. It was sometimes called a "lily" in the Bible, because the garlic plant is a member of the lily family. The onion plant is a similar member.

大蒜是種非常古老的植物。我們可以在很多古書裡看到它。在聖經中，有時稱它爲「百合花」，因爲大蒜是百合花科的一員。洋蔥也是同一家族的成員。

Both the garlic and onion plants have a very strong odor,

大蒜和洋蔥的氣味都非常強烈，

**

lily〔ˈlɪlɪ〕*n.* 百合花　ancient〔ˈenʃənt〕*adj.* 古代的
times〔taɪmz〕*n. pl.* 時代　Egypt〔ˈidʒɪpt〕*n.* 埃及
garlic〔ˈgɑrlɪk〕*n.* 大蒜　crave〔krev〕*v.* 渴望　place〔ples〕*v.* 放置
neck〔nɛk〕*n.* 脖子　string〔strɪŋ〕*n.* 線　***keep away*** 使遠離
luck〔lʌk〕*n.* 運氣　Bible〔ˈbaɪbl̩〕*n.* 聖經
member〔ˈmɛmbɚ〕*n.* 成員　onion〔ˈʌnjən〕*n.* 洋蔥
similar〔ˈsɪmələ˞〕*adj.* 類似的；同樣的　odor〔ˈodɚ〕*n.* 氣味

but garlic's smell is much stronger than onion's. Many claim that garlic's smell is the strongest smell among all foods.

但是大蒜的味道比洋蔥還強烈。許多人宣稱大蒜的味道是所有食物裡最強烈的。

Many folks today think that garlic is beneficial to the health. They believe that it prevents illness.

現在許多人認爲大蒜有益健康。他們相信大蒜可以預防疾病。

Garlic may benefit us in one way. Its strong smell may keep away people. Because of this it may stop people from spreading germs to each other. It is not easy at all to eliminate the smell of garlic.

大蒜可能在某方面對我們有益。它強烈的味道使人退避三舍。因此可以阻止人們把細菌散播給對方。要消除大蒜的氣味並不容易。

For decades people have tried to handle it. But all efforts have been in vain. Now, we know the reason why.

幾十年來，人們試著去對付它。但所有的努力都白費了。我們現在才知道原因。

The smell of garlic goes into the lungs. From there it comes out. It comes out through the skin, too.

大蒜的氣味會跑進肺裡。它會從肺跑出來，也會透過皮膚跑出來。

**

smell (smɛl) *n.* 氣味　claim (klem) *v.* 宣稱　folks (foks) *n.pl.* 人們
beneficial (ˌbɛnəˈfɪʃəl) *adj.* 有益的　health (hɛlθ) *n.* 健康
prevent (prɪˈvɛnt) *v.* 預防　illness (ˈɪlnɪs) *n.* 疾病
benefit (ˈbɛnəfɪt) *v.* 有益於　***in one way*** 在某方面　stop (stɑp) *v.* 阻止
spread (sprɛd) *v.* 散播　germ (dʒɝm) *n.* 細菌
eliminate (ɪˈlɪməˌnet) *v.* 消除　decade (ˈdɛked) *n.* 十年
handle (ˈhændḷ) *v.* 對付；處理　effort (ˈɛfɚt) *n.* 努力
in vain 白費地　reason (ˈrizṇ) *n.* 理由　lung (lʌŋ) *n.* 肺
through (θru) *prep.* 透過　skin (skɪn) *n.* 皮膚

銘傳大學 97 學年度全校英語演講比賽

比賽目的	提升學生英文程度及學習英語之興趣。
比賽項目	即席演講
參加對象	具中華民國國籍或過去十年未曾在以英語為母語之國家或地區求學或居住累積達六個月以上之在校生
題目與規則	於當天命題，當場抽題，上台前 3 分鐘進入「準備室」準備。
評分標準	發音及語調佔 25%　流利度佔 25% 肢體語言佔 10%　內容組織佔 30% 台風＋整體表現佔 10%
計時方式	演講者開始講話或有表演動作即開始計時，二分三十秒時舉黃牌提示，滿三分鐘舉紅牌，同時按鈴以示結束。

國立暨台灣省公私立高級中等學校 96 學年度學生英語演講比賽

比賽目的	培育 e 世代外語人才，提升高中學生英語文程度，增進學生英語表達能力。
比賽項目	看圖即席演講
參加對象	國立暨台灣省公私立高級中等學校普通科學生
題目與規則	由主辦單位聘請命題委員命擬，於決賽時當場公布決定，準備時間為五分鐘，學生登台演講前不得與他人接觸。
評分標準	內容佔 30%　語言能力佔 30% 表達技巧佔 30%　儀態佔 10%
計時方式	演講時間以二分鐘為限；一分半鐘為一短鈴，二分鐘為一長鈴，滿兩分鐘，立即結束。

台北縣三重市五華國民小學 96 學年度英語競賽

比賽目的	加強本校英語教育，提高兒童英語學習興趣，展現學習成效。
比賽項目	看圖說故事
參加對象	五、六年級學生
題目與規則	1. 事前公佈 2 幅四格漫畫。 2. 比賽當天由承辦單位備圖，專人替換。 3. 不可帶稿。 4. 不可使用任何擴音設備。 5. 參賽者須於競賽前 10 分鐘抽題，於準備區就坐。
評分標準	語音 45%（音準、語調、聲韻） 內容 45%（思想、結構、詞彙） 儀態 10%（儀容、態度、表情）
計時方式	演講限時 3 分鐘，2 分鐘按第一次鈴，3 分鐘按第二次鈴即結束。

台北縣三重市碧華國民小學 95 學年度語文教育競賽

比賽目的	落實語文教育，提高語文研究及學習興趣，並蔚爲風氣，而收弘揚文化績效。
比賽項目	英語看圖說故事
參加對象	五、六年級學生
題目與規則	競賽員自行就教務處事前公布題目中擇 1 上臺參賽。
評分標準	語音 45%（音準、語調、聲韻） 內容 45%（思想、結構、詞彙） 儀態 10%（儀容、態度、表情）
計時方式	演講時間爲 2~3 分鐘，2 分鐘一到按第 1 次鈴，3 分鐘按第 2 次，時間超過或不足時，每半分鐘扣 1 分，未足半分鐘，以半分鐘計。

彰化縣消防局 95 年度英語看圖說故事比賽

比賽目的	爲提高彰化縣消防人員學習英語興趣，並營造優質英語學習環境，激起各單位消防人員學習英文動力，培養爲未來每人第二專長語言，並皆能通過全民英文檢定測驗初級以上測驗，致使消防爲民服務工作能與國際觀光趨勢接軌，有效提昇消防爲民服務優良形象。
比賽項目	英語看圖說故事
參加對象	內勤各業務課、室、中心人員及各外勤消防大隊人員
題目與規則	參加人員自行準備單篇或連環圖片，並影印數份供現場展示、評審、觀眾觀賞。每人準備時間 20 分鐘。
評分標準	內容 40%　語音 20%　語調 20% 儀態 15%　時間 5%
計時方式	演講時間 3 分鐘

臺北市立明倫高級中學 94 學年度英文作文暨英語演講比賽

比賽目的	加強英文教育，提高學生研習英文之興趣，增進學生英語寫作及英語表達能力，並選拔代表參加臺北市比賽。
比賽項目	看圖即席演講
參加對象	高一、高二學生
題目與規則	採看圖說故事方式，題目當場抽籤決定，準備時間 5 分鐘。
評分標準	內容 40%　語言表達能力 40% 儀態 20%
計時方式	演說時間爲 2 分鐘，時間超過或不足時，每 30 秒扣總平均分數 1 分，未足 30 秒以 30 秒計。

國立新店高級中學94學年度高二英語演講暨英文作文比賽

比賽目的	促進英文科教學之生動活潑，加強本校同學英語演說及英文寫作能力，以提高英語文程度。
比賽項目	英語演講
參加對象	高二學生
題目與規則	採看圖說故事方式，圖片由籌備小組老師準備，於比賽準備時間公布。準備時間爲六分鐘，於登台演講前不得與他人交談。
評分標準	內容40%　語言表達能力40% 儀態10%　時間10%
計時方式	演說時間爲2分鐘

台南縣私立港明高中88學年度英語文競賽

比賽目的	鼓勵本校師生加強英語文教、學，提高對英語文研習興趣，以蔚爲風氣，並據以拔擢優秀人才，以利往後派出校外參賽。
比賽項目	看圖說故事
參加對象	國三學生
題目與規則	圖片由英語文教學研究會負責。賽前十五天交由教學組公佈，並於比賽前抽題之用。
評分標準	發音及語調50%　內容30% 氣勢與儀態（儀容、態度、表情）20%。
計時方式	各組每人均限二分半鐘，時間一到按鈴警告，不足或超過時間每三十秒扣一分。不足或超過三十秒，以三十秒計。中途停頓時間長達一分鐘者，立即按鈴下台並扣分。

桃園縣私立振聲高級中學87學年度第二學期高中英語看圖說故事比賽

比賽目的	提高學生學習英語興趣，增進英文之學習效果。
比賽項目	英語看圖說故事
參加對象	高一學生
題目與規則	比賽圖片由英文科教學研究會討論決定。比賽當日，抽籤四選一進行比賽。

用英文說故事①

主　　編／劉　毅

發 行 所／學習出版有限公司　☎ (02) 2704-5525

郵撥帳號／0512727-2 學習出版社帳戶

登 記 證／局版台業 2179 號

印 刷 所／裕強彩色印刷有限公司

台北門市／台北市許昌街 10 號 2 F　☎ (02) 2331-4060・2331-9209

台灣總經銷／紅螞蟻圖書有限公司　☎ (02) 2795-3656

美國總經銷／Evergreen Book Store　☎ (818) 2813622

本公司網址 www.learnbook.com.tw

電子郵件 learnbook@learnbook.com.tw

售價：新台幣二百八十元正

2009 年 3 月 1 日新修訂

ISBN 978-957-519-932-6

結語 1

That's the end.

My story stops there.

Did you enjoy it?

結 語 ❷

The story ends right here.

How did you like it?

Do you have any questions?

結語 ❸

That's all there is.

That's the end of the story.

What did you think of it?

結 語 ④

My story is over.

Did you like how it ended?

Did you find it interesting?